# THE
# FORGIVEN

# THE
# FORGIVEN

Mike Shepherd

# THE FORGIVEN

*iUniverse books may be ordered through booksellers or by contacting:*

*iUniverse*
*1663 Liberty Drive*
*Bloomington, IN 47403*
*www.iuniverse.com*
*1-800-Authors (1-800-288-4677)*

*Because of the dynamic nature of the Internet, any web addresses or links contained in this book may have changed since publication and may no longer be valid. The views expressed in this work are solely those of the author and do not necessarily reflect the views of the publisher, and the publisher hereby disclaims any responsibility for them.*

*Any people depicted in stock imagery provided by Thinkstock are models, and such images are being used for illustrative purposes only. Certain stock imagery © Thinkstock.*

*ISBN: 978-1-5320-2670-6 (sc)*
*ISBN: 978-1-5320-2671-3 (e)*

*Print information available on the last page.*

*iUniverse rev. date:   06/21/2017*

# CHAPTER 1

One of the earliest memories of my mother and me was when we listened to Don McNeil's Breakfast Club on the radio in the kitchen together while she made pancakes before sending me off to school after dad had already gone to work.

In can still see her standing in the doorway, waving goodbye. It always brought me to tears. I hated leaving her. I was a real momma's boy. But that all changed when she suddenly became an alcoholic. She seemed to change overnight into a Jekyll and Hyde under the influence of a diabolic potion. She went from being a laid back, loving housewife and mother to a drunken maniac. Had she just been bored? Or was there something in her background that would have led to such behavior? I didn't know. I only knew that she was making the lives of me and my two little sisters miserable. One night in particular the drunken spatting between my parents became so intense I left the house and took refuge in a drainage ditch nearby where I was attacked by a couple of rats that I fended off with a stick. I stayed outside until sunrise then I went back in to get ready for school. Mom and Dad were passed out and my sisters were curled up in bed together sleeping. I woke them, we got dressed and went to school on empty stomachs with very little sleep. It was difficult to concentrate, much less stay awake, after what I'd been through the night before – after what I'd been through many nights before -- and my grades suffered.

Sometimes in the middle of the night Dad would have to call an ambulance to take Mom to the hospital to have her stomach pumped because she had overdosed on booze and pills. Then he, too, became an alcoholic, and our lives became even more chaotic. Mother's suicide attempts became more frequent. One night we knocked a tall glass of iodine from her lips, and pulled her head out of the oven whose pilot light wasn't lit, as gas filled the room. Confirming the old adage that no good deed goes unpunished. Her angry response to my saving her life, was to shower me with dishes from the cabinets. I huddled beneath the kitchen table to avoid being hit on the head. Because of her insane behavior we locked her out. But she smashed her fist through the glass window of the door, while screaming that she was going to light a match and blow the place up with everybody in it. The neighbors in the adjoining apartment heard the commotion and called the police, who took her to the hospital for stitches, then committed her to the psych ward. My paternal grandparents took us in because my dad, overwhelmed by the situation, had a nervous breakdown of his own.

I vividly recall the first morning I woke up at my grandparents house. The sweet summer sun shone through the breeze-blown lace curtains, and for the first time in a long time I felt secure.

# CHAPTER 2

Life with grandma and grandpa was as predictable as the band concerts on Main Street every Saturday night, and church every Sunday morning. What we didn't predict, however, was mother pounding on the door one gloomy, rainy Monday, demanding that my sisters and me be returned to her. She insisted that she was sober now, and capable of caring for us like a mother was supposed to do – not grandparents – so we were forced to go with her because she was our legal guardian.

We lived with her in an apartment above a tavern, a location not conducive to sobriety, and she soon started drinking again, and carousing with men who she'd bring home to screw . One of them was a big, mean sonofabitch named Dennis, who knocked her around. He didn't confine his brutality to women. Jealous of Mom's past relationship with my father, who also lived above a tavern nearby, he wanted her to prove her love for him by convincing her to invite Dad to the tavern downstairs for a drink so Dennis could ambush him, and he did with a ball bat, knocking Dad's teeth out and splitting his lip up to his eye. It required forty stitches to close.

After they got out of jail -- Mom was charged with conspiracy – Dennis and Mom jumped bail and left town together, and Dad moved in with us. Later we heard that Dennis robbed a bank in Washington state and was doing time in Walla Walla prison. What became of mom we didn't know -- and didn't care.

Like a dog abused as a puppy, I grew into an angry young man and I took it out on some of my classmates in high school, on the football field. I became a vicious middle linebacker (although I was small), but my grades weren't good enough to go on to college. After barely graduating, I went to work as a landscaper for a tree nursery. On the weekends I went camping by myself in the woods by a lake on the outskirts of town. After a while I became bored with the same old routine. Although alcoholism had destroyed my childhood, I took some beer and a pint of apricot brandy along, and I got drunk for the first time in my life. I ran wild through a stand of pines, and quickly discovered that human flesh was no match for tree bark. I sustained serious abrasions all over my face. Monday morning one of the girls who worked with herbal plants in the greenhouse smeared aloe vera gel on the wounds and they quickly healed. A relationship between the two of us developed, even though

I was a little bitter toward women, because of my mom, I suppose. Conversely, Rose Marie had been deserted by her father and she was a little bitter toward men, I discovered, so the feeling was mutual, especially when we were drinking. But we managed to get along fairly well when we were sober, which was about half of the time.

Meanwhile the Vietnam War was escalating and guys were getting drafted left and right. Uncle Sam's fateful finger was pointed directly at me, so to avoid having to go into the infantry I joined the Air Force hoping to avoid combat in 'Nam. Despite poor grades in high school I scored high in English aptitude on the Air Force entry exam and was invited to attend Armed Forces Journalism School. Upon graduating, out of a class of 50 I was the only one with orders for Vietnam – my punishment for finishing last in the class. So away I went, along with 200 other shave-tailed nephews of Uncle Sam, soaring off into the wild blue yonder.

Taking off at sundown in a pink Braniff jet, I glanced back at San Francisco, partially shrouded in blue-gray mist. The Golden Gate Bridge, spanning the city's skyline, appeared as a crown on the head of a queen watching her knights depart for a distant war. As I turned away, I caught a glimpse of light glowing softly in a tower on a hill. It looked like a tear.

Settling in for the long flight to Vietnam, I wondered, which of us would not return? The baby-faced kid sitting next to me? The black guy across the aisle? He was smiling with his eyes closed. Maybe he was thinking about a girlfriend, a wife and kids, his mother, or the joke his father told him last night over a farewell beer. Or the loudmouthed jerk behind me who was yakking about how many "slant-eyed gooks" he'd kill. The Asian-American Marine sitting next to him? Me?

I gazed at my reflection in the window. Mom used to say I looked like Van Johnson, the war movie hero, with my reddish-blond hair, blue eyes and smattering of freckles, but now I thought I looked more like some scared little kid on his way to the dentist. I could see fear in my eyes – fear of the unknown, and of what awaited me on the other side of the big pond.

We leveled off at 45,000 feet above the Pacific and sped for 'Nam in a race with the sun in a futile attempt to prolong our last day of innocence. It was a race that we ultimately lost when the sea swallowed the last glint of light. We drifted all night, farther and farther away from home, and for some (perhaps me) there'd be no return.

While falling asleep, I thought about my girlfriend Rose Marie, who I last saw standing on the porch in the gloomy gray dawn just a day and a half before, waving goodbye. It seemed so long ago, like another lifetime in another world.

# CHAPTER 3

It didn't take me long to see action as a radio news correspondent for 7th Air Force Information. I was assigned to cover the siege of Khe Sanh in January of 1968, then my next assignment took me into the hotly-contested A Shau Valley to interview the troops there about the effectiveness of air support.

It was customary for those of us who worked in Da Nang's Air Force radio news office to go to the NCO Club for happy hour every night. Sometimes we stayed later, though, on Saturday nights when we didn't have to work the next day. But this Sunday would be different. I'd be going into the valley on the first plane to land there in some time, which made it worthy of a story. An artery of the Ho Chi Minh Trail ran down the middle of the valley, from around the DMZ through Laos before it branched out into South Vietnam. After fierce fighting with the North Vietnamese Army, the American 1st Cavalry Division took control of it and its airstrip. This is where I'd be landing on a C-130 loaded with ammo -- an easy target for the enemy antiaircraft guns in the hills surrounding the valley. Fearing that I'd be shot down, I continued drinking, thinking each beer could be my last, and I was well on my way to getting drunk. I awoke in the morning with a rip-roaring hangover. After wiping the sleep from my eyes, I glanced at the clock.

"Oh shit! That plane leaves in twenty minutes!" I was a good twenty minutes from the terminal. I quickly grabbed a tape recorder and tapes, a holster and a .38 pistol, which we were required to carry when flying, and rushed out the door. By the time I got to the terminal, the plane had already taken off, so I went to the office and sat at my desk with hung over head in hands, waiting for my boss to arrive. When he came in and saw me sitting there, the shit hit the fan.

"You missed that god damn plane, didn't you?"

"I'm sorry, Joe"

"You're a sorry drunk." His eyes flared with anger.

"Out all night drinking, and you overslept, right? Well you blew the assignment. As far as I'm concerned you can...."

Just then the red phone rang.

"Jesus Christ Almighty!" Joe said over the phone after a moment of listening. "No, sir, he wasn't on it. Yes, sir, he missed it. In two hours? Yes, sir, I'll make sure he's on it.

"Well, Mick, you lucked out, big time. The plane you were supposed to have been on was shot down going into the valley. Blown to bits, no survivors. That means the next one going in will still be the first one, and you'll be on it. It leaves in two hours. Be there early."

The time I had to spare gave me more than enough time to think about how close I had come to dying. I had missed the ill-fated flight by a mere ten minutes or so, a relatively small window in time through which I could have lived or died. While waiting for the plane, I drifted off into a state of semi-consciousness, and I had the strangest sensation that I was in a twilight zone, somewhere between life and death.

"Airman Scott, Airman Scott!"

"Huh?'

I looked up. The sergeant behind the counter was calling my name.

"That plane for A Shau Valley is ready to go," he said. "Better hurry. It's that C-130 right our there."

After what felt like about half an hour, we began to descend rather abruptly, and the crew chief told me to fasten my seat belt tightly. We were dropping into A Shau Valley quickly, instead of a long low approach, in an attempt to avoid enemy antiaircraft fire.

Suddenly there was a terrific jolt, and I braced myself as we touched down hard on the tarmac. The pilot reversed the engines and we roared toward the end of the runway. After we came to a stop, the rear cargo door dropped down, and I got off of the plane. The crew began to offload the ammo with a fork lift they'd brought along.

I looked around for some grunts to talk to about the importance of this re-supply mission, and the significance of the first plane to land in the valley in a while, thanks to their kicking the NVA out of the valley. A 1st Cav lieutenant intercepted me and ordered me to fall in with a group of men standing by. It turned out to be a detail to recover bodies -- or what was left of them – from the strewn wreckage of the plane that had been shot down. Apparently because I was wearing a US military uniform in a war zone I was not exempt from such details even though I was an Air Force newsie.

"Fan out through the grass and those trees," he said. "Look for dog tags and wallets, anything that could identify the bodies and body parts."

Feeling as if I were still in the twilight zone between life and death that I had imagined at the air terminal, I wandered like a zombie among the smoldering wreckage of the plane. There was a seat attached to a fragment of fuselage hanging in a tree with a badly burned dead man in it. There were pieces of the plane and body parts scattered about for the next hundred yards. As I continued walking, I stumbled over what I first thought was a log. When I looked back I saw that it was the charred torso of a man. It could have been mine if I hadn't gotten drunk and missed the ill-fated plane.

My life had been spared long enough to read the Dear John from Rose Marie that was waiting for me when I returned to Da Nang.

In recognition of the trauma I recently experienced, which included being under fire at Khe Sanh, Joe recommended that I take an R&R, to which I gladly consented. I chose to go to Sydney, Australia. He had been there on his R&R.

"The people down there love Americans," he said. "They're forever grateful for our keeping the Japs off their backs in World War II."

Two days later I was flying over the Equator, seven miles above Borneo, and roughly halfway between Saigon and Sydney. It didn't feel any different than flying over other superficial milestones, like the Continental Divide or the International Dateline. Not the slightest glitch or tinge of turbulence, nor difference in the color of the sky and seas did I detect, as we transcended hemispheres.

When we landed in Sydney, before disembarking, a US Army Special Services representative came onboard to discuss the social behavior expected of us in Australia. He was a master of euphemisms.

"Listen up, gentlemen," he said. "There are plenty of wholesome Australian women here who like to, shall we say, date GIs, so it will not be necessary to contract for professional companionship. However, please be advised, in either case, as a precautionary measure it would be wise to procure prophylactic devices should opportunities to copulate arise."

We were then whisked away by a bus to an R&R reception center in downtown Sydney to make reservations for hotels, and to be fitted for civilian clothes if we hadn't brought our own. Wearing US military uniforms on R&R was not permitted. Apparently the Vietnam War had become unpopular with some in Australia, particularly among the growing hippie population in Sydney. We were advised to keep a low profile to avoid confrontations. Our GI haircuts alone were dead giveaways, which in some cases would be to our advantage, but not always, as I would soon discover.

After making reservations at a small hotel called the Auburn House, I went to a reception at the Sheraton Hotel where dozens of young Australian women greeted us. They were very friendly and didn't hesitate to engage us in small talk. Most of us hadn't been around women for a while (except for those who patronized the bar girls in Vietnam who boozed them up and talked them into having sex for a price). With these Aussie girls, the hustle was a little more subtle. Although there was plenty of booze at the reception, nobody appeared to be talking sex, at least yet.

A rock'n'roll band played, and people danced. With each drink and song, more GIs and girls formed couples until the last dance, when I found myself to be the last man out. Some things never change: I was still getting my ass kicked at musical chairs, so I arranged for a cab to take me to my hotel, a five storey glass building with balconies on a hill overlooking Bondi Beach. The Pacific Ocean rolled in below, with surfers riding its waves. A strong breeze, laden with the scent of the sea, blew against me as I walked, suitcase in hand, to the front door. I was rather tipsy from the beer I drank at the reception, and I needed to lie down, so I checked in and went to my room, lay down and went to sleep. When I awoke I took a shower and dressed, called a cab and went to the lobby to wait. While waiting, I picked up a brochure from a table and looked it over. On the cover was a panoramic photo of Bondi Beach, stretching to Sydney Harbor in the distance, where the iconic Opera House, framed by the arching Harbor Bridge, resembled a flotilla of sailboats moored on the waterfront. The city's rising skyline was also visible. It was a breathtaking view that rivaled San Francisco's.

The text of the brochure described Sydney as "*laid back, soft and warm, like her bikini clad beauties basking in the sun on endless South Sea beaches. At times she is daring and shows off, like the surfers hanging ten on the big waves, and she's dazzling as the colorful sails of ritzy yachts plying the tropical waters.*

"*Uptown, in the parks, lunch timers lie in the shade of palms and eucalyptus trees, while lawn bowlers play their gentle game on manicured grass, as the self-righteous on soap box pedestals rail about the Vietnam War and other topics of the day.*

"*Sydney is proud, up front, and loud and clear as the ocean crashing against her jagged cliffs on wild, stormy nights.*

"*The nightlife of the city centers around Kings Cross, the entertainment district, where in the private clubs and pubs, champagne-sipping socialites rub elbows with beer-drinking cowboys on holiday from the bush, and American servicemen on leave from Vietnam – a mix that makes the 'Cross' unique.*"

Kings cross sounded like the place for me. As soon as I got out of the cab and before I could get into a bar, I was accosted by two hippie chicks and a dude with a black and white peace sign painted on his entire face.

Apparently they had heard my American accent when I talked to the cabbie.

"Get out of Vietnam! Fuck your bombs and napalm!" they shouted, "get out of Sydney! Baby killer! What makes you think you're welcome here?"

I was so taken aback that I didn't know what to say. I tried to get away, but they followed me, nipping at my heels like dogs, barking their antiwar, anti-American diatribe. I ducked into a bar. They started to come in after me, but apparently the bartender knew they were trouble. He shooed them away at the door.

"Hounding you about the war?" he asked.

"Yes."

"Yeah, well that's their routine. Can I get you a drink?'

"I'll have a beer, a Foster's – that's the only Australian beer I know."

He served me the beer, along with a complimentary bowl of mixed nuts. I gobbled up a few handfuls in lieu of supper, and washed them down with one beer, then another. I was trying to settle my nerves, which were a little frayed from my encounter with the hippies.

"I didn't expect to encounter so much animosity about the war here in Sydney," I said to the bartender.

"There are some who are against it, but most Australians support it, I think. I do, for sure. To be quite honest, it's good for business having you Americans here for R&R."

I looked around. Judging from the haircuts and conversation I overheard, in voices without Aussie accents, quite a few GIs were in the bar. What the bar lacked, however, was women, so I headed for another bar in search of the female companionship the special services representative said was so plentiful in Sydney. Before leaving, I peeked outside to see if the hippies were still there. They had gone, so I moved on. I was soon approached in the middle of the block by two flamboyantly-dressed street walkers. They looked like twins. They competed for my attention by playfully rubbing their bodies against mine, and whispering into my ear the price of certain sex acts, including the price for both of them. I was tempted, but I recalled what I'd been told, that there were plenty of wholesome Australian women to date for free. I still hoped for that, so I broke away from the hookers.

The next bar I came to had a flier on the door advertising a rock 'n' roll band called the Kangaroos. I could hear them from out on the street, and they sounded pretty good, so I went in.

There were women dancing, some with men and some with each other. It looked like the place for me. I found a stool at the bar, sat down, and ordered a Foster's. What else? After another, I got up enough nerve to go to a table at which four women sat, to ask one of them to dance. In unison they told me to "...fuck off GI!"

After this, and my encounter with the hippies, I got the distinct impression that GIs and the Vietnam War weren't very popular in Sydney, so I kept a low profile for the rest of my R&R.

# CHAPTER 4

After I returned to the States and was discharged from the Air Force, I enrolled at Southern Illinois University at Carbondale on the GI Bill. It had a well-earned reputation for being a party school, but it was also a haven for hippies, and a hotbed for the antiwar movement. There were also many returning veterans like myself, which made for an interesting mix of students.

As to partying, ex-GIs did plenty of that at a bar called The Club. Women went there too, and after my experience in Australia, it was nice to know that they liked us. I soon met the acquaintance of a townie named Trudy. When we first met she asked me the basics: "where ya from, "who's your favorite group," and "what's your sign?"

"Springfield, the Young Rascals, Scorpio," I replied.

"Scorpio?" she responded smiling, and she lifted an eyebrow and made a clicking sound with her tongue against her teeth.

"The sign of sex," she said bluntly.

"Really? Since when?

We both laughed.

"And death," she added. "Ruled by the planet Pluto. It's one of the water signs. Scorpes have a strong feminine side too." Something I didn't particularly like hearing, being kind of macho, but I liked hearing Trudy talk. She had a sweet, southern Illinois accent. Carbondale was closer to Memphis than Chicago, sparing her that unpleasant twang, which I was sure that I had, being from the plains of central Illinois.

"What's your sign?" I asked in return.

"Aquarius," she said with apparent pride.

"So what are Aquarians all about?"

"Compassion, mostly, but right now I'm a thirsty Aquarian. I need a drink."

When I stood up to let her out of the booth we were sitting in, my eyes followed her as she made her way through the crowd to the bar. Her tall, slender, well-shaped figure moved gracefully and she left a trace of perfume behind that I recognized as patchouli oil, which was what Chelsea wore.

Chelsea was the last woman I had been with, in July in San Francisco, the night I got back from Vietnam. I had met her in Haight-Ashbury while wandering around half-drunk, like a tourist wanting to see what real hippies looked like up close, and I literally stumbled upon one sitting on a curb – Chelsea, and she got me stoned on hash and we wound up body surfing together on her waterbed. Those waves had long petered out and I was marooned on dry sand. It was high time to get wet again.

I laughed to myself about my lewd, double entendre musings, but I was serious about my intentions. I fully intended to live up to the Zodiacal characteristics Trudy said were peculiar to Scorpios, excluding the death aspect, unless I died doing it with her, which I fantasized about while watching her walk to the bar. Her long blond hair fell down her back, and my eyes followed it to her hips. While waiting for the drinks, she subtly moved her hips to the music playing on the juke box; a slow, jazzy sensuous tune featuring a sexy saxophone.

When she returned with her drink and sat back down, I cozied up to her, and she responded in kind. Soon we were kissing and oblivious to anyone else around. We had become acquainted fast, which was the trend in this age of fly-by-night sex. I asked her if she wanted to go some place else more private. My place was what I had in mind, but she had other plans.

"My place would be nice," she whispered, close to my ear.

We got up and went outside. I took a deep breath, and at once, the cool autumn air intensified the high I felt from the alcohol.

"Ahhh, what a rush!"

The sidewalk was crowded, and we stepped back against the front of the bar to avoid being swept along.

"Where you parked?" Trudy asked.

"I walked tonight," I said.

"I'm parked over there." We walked across the street to a yellow Volkswagen beetle. She unlocked the door, let me in and we drove off. Confined to such a small space without drinks we both became a little shy and conversed somewhat nervously about trivial things. Six blocks west of Illinois Avenue, she turned up a long, worn, gravel lane to the back of a wooded lot where a little green trailer sat, lighted by a lamp on a utility pole which shone amidst a sugar maple whose bright yellow leaves, some falling, gave off a dried, musty smell – the smell of autumn.

"Home sweet home," Trudy said.

This was her home away from home in Carbondale, she told me. Her parents lived on the outskirts of town, but being devout, church-going folk, they didn't approve of her lifestyle, so she had moved out her senior year in high school – the year before. She was only 18 and worked as a waitress at a diner. Bartenders didn't care if she wasn't 21; she looked it.

As soon as we stepped inside the trailer I could see that the place was strictly decorated in astrology motifs. The walls were adorned with black light posters of psychedelic green, purple, blue, pink, orange and yellow Gothic art representing the twelve Zodiac signs. The mystical new wave music Trudy played added to the cosmic atmosphere.

"Have a seat," Trudy said, motioning to the couch. She lit a stick of incense and some candles, then went to the kitchenette and came back with two glasses and a bottle of wine, which she placed on the coffee table. She opened a small wooden box and produced a joint, assuming that I partook. We smoked and drank and Trudy spoke of astrology, of course, and how compatible Scorpios and Aquarians were, especially when the sun is in such-and-such position and this planet is aligned with that one and it's in retrograde. The thought of all of it, along with the wine, pot and incense smoke and new wave music made my head swim. I sat back and Trudy placed her hand softly against my cheek. "Let's go where it's more comfortable."

She took my hand and led me into the bedroom where we undressed, lay down and after much creative foreplay made love until we were both satisfied – as satisfied as two stoned people could be. We then fell asleep, and in the morning I slipped away without waking Trudy, and walked home in the crisp autumn dawn, my favorite time of year, when the Sun in is Scorpio, the sign of sex.

Not all of the women who came to The Club were necessarily pro-vet, as I would eventually find out, although they initially seemed to be. On Halloween night, while smoking a joint in the alley behind the bar with a small group of people, it was handed to me by a woman who happened by. I couldn't tell if she was a hippie or just dressed up like a gypsy for Halloween. She had dark hair like a gypsy would have, but her eyes, visible from moonlight, were blue, and her skin was white.

After a few tokes she exclaimed, "Wow, this is some dynamite shit!"

"Yeah, we call it "Nam bomb,'" one of the guys smoking said.

"Were you guys in Vietnam?" she inquired.

I really didn't want to think or talk about Vietnam tonight. Sometimes it made me angry, and I didn't want to be angry -- not on my birthday which began at midnight -- but I answered her question anyway.

"Yeah." Then I tried to change the subject. "What's your name?" I asked.

"Cathy."

She wouldn't let me change the subject.

"Must be pretty bad over there, huh?"

"Yeah. So where ya from, Cathy?"

"St. Louis. Did you kill anyone?"

"No."

"What branch were you in?"

"Air Force."

"Oh, the bombers. Drop any napalm?"

"Me? No, I wasn't a pilot."

The tone of the conversation was changing, and I knew where it was headed.

"I saw a photograph in a magazine of children screaming as they ran down the road from a Vietnamese village after it had been hit by that shit," Cathy said, her big blue eyes peering intensely at mine, as if I were responsible. "Seems like an awful lot of innocent people are getting hurt by that fucked up war."

"That's right," I shot back. "Thousands were executed by Communist forces at Hue because they chose not to side with them when the Tet Offensive of '68 began."

I could feel my temperature rising. "Hey, what the hell, did you stop here to pick a fight?"

"No. I'm sorry." She smiled and put her hand on my arm. "I guess I got a little carried away. Hey, would you like to go to a Halloween party?"

I looked around. The little pot party had fizzled out. With the joint smoked, the others had gone inside.

"Uh, sure, why not."

"Wanna walk?" Cathy asked. It's not too far."

"Okay."

It was a blustery night. Most of the leaves had fallen from the trees by now, and some of them were blowing across the street making skit-scat-skittering sounds. A dog barked; it sounded large, and chills ran up my spine. Halloween was in the air.

"So where's this party?" I asked.

"Bucky's dome."

"Bucky's dome?"

"Buckminister Fuller," Cathy said incredulously. "Surely you've heard of him. The world-famous architect? He's a design professor here."

"Oh yeah. He built that brown thing at the corner of Forest and Cherry."

"That's the one."

Coincidently I lived across the street from it. Soon we were there. I looked over at my house and in one of the windows my black cat sat puffed up and looking perfectly Halloweenish; yellow eyes glowing like a jack-o-lantern's. I pointed him out to Cathy.

"Far out," she said with a snicker.

I looked at the dome. I had grown accustomed to seeing it every day going to and from campus, but tonight, stoned as I was, its globular, multi-faceted, brown shingled facade resembled a large exotic mushroom growing in the moonlight, with classical music wafting from inside.

I followed Cathy through the door. It appeared so much larger on the inside, and at once I felt as if I had stepped into another world.

The interior was lighted by sconces, and a singular moon-like globe hanging from the center of the ceiling directly above a large round table with a punch bowl where people, dressed in a variety of costumes, milled about.

Suddenly I realized Cathy had left me alone, so I made my way to the punch bowl for a little social lubrication. As I ladled a glass of the punch, not the least bit concerned about what it might contain, I thought I heard someone faintly calling my name. I looked around and spotted my roomy Jan standing off by himself. He nodded at me and smiled. It was nice to see a familiar face; one that wasn't made up or masked. Other than Cathy's, Jan's appeared to be the only one that wasn't. Oh yes, and mine. I sauntered over to Jan.

"What's happening, Timothy?" I asked, referring to the guru Leary, who he had dressed as before we left the house and went our separate ways. I had no idea this was the party he was attending.

"Everything, man, everything is happening everywhere you are when you're hip to being there," was his reply to my rhetorical question.

"Well, I guess that pretty much covers it," I said. "So, which one of these creatures is Fuller?"

"Oh, Bucky's in Boston." Jan knew this because he was in the design program. "His assistant is throwing the party. That's him over there, dressed like Raggedy Ann."

"Okay."

"So what brings you to this party, Mick? I thought you were going to The Club tonight?"

"Some little hippie chick. That's her at the punch bowl. I met her at The Club."

"Oh shit, that's Cathy Riggins, she's in design too. What the fuck was she doing there? She hates vets. Damn, here she comes now. I'm gone, man, I don't wanna talk to her when I'm trippin', or any other time for that matter, about that fucked up war." Apparently Jan had experienced her wrath, also being a veteran of Vietnam.

Jan quickly got lost in the crowd as Cathy, who was drunk, came straight to me and got into my face about what else, Vietnam. She sounded like the Communist broadcast propagandist, Hanoi Hannah, who I'd heard many times on the radio over there.

"You imperialist warmongering air pirate pig. How can you drop napalm on innocent children and kill old men and women? How can you justify poisoning the countryside with Agent Orange, and turning Vietnamese housewives and teenage girls into whores for the pleasure of marauding GIs who murder their husbands and fathers?"

She was all over me like a yapping little dog (reminiscent of the hippies I had encountered in Sidney), and I backed away not knowing what to say. I soon found myself backing out the door, then Jan came outside, having seen what had happened.

"I told ya, man, that chick hates vets."

Stunned by the suddenness and violence of it all, I shivered with anger that guys like Jan and me were being treated so badly by snotty little hippie chicks like Cathy.

As time went by, the anger inside of me festered like an ulcer in my stomach, which led to excessive drinking in a futile attempt to numb the pain; it only made matters worse. I spent more time at The Club and other bars than in the classroom, and I soon went on academic probation. To address the situation, my guidance counselor called me in for consultation. He knew that I was a vet, and he was one too; of the Korean War. Because of my drinking and anger, he concluded that I was finding it difficult to readjust.

"It's being diagnosed as PTSD -- post traumatic stress disorder," he said. "If you'd like, I can arrange for you to get some counseling for it at a vets' center in Marion."

I was reluctant at first, but the alternative would be to flunk out of school, so I decided to go. The counselor there addressed the drinking first. "It's one of the symptoms of PTSD," she said.

"But I was drinking a lot before I went to Vietnam."

"Is there alcoholism in your family?"

"Both of my parents."

Revealing this opened the door on my tumultuous childhood, and she determined that, as a result of this, I suffered from an early onset of PTSD, which was only aggravated by my Vietnam experience. The drinking aggravates the condition, she said. She suggested that I attend AA meetings. I thought I was too young for that, so I decided to try to quit on my own. It worked for a while, until spring, when outdoor rock concerts took place at nearby Giant City State Park, and I went along with the crowd, smoking dope and drinking cheap wine.

Ironically the Vet's Club sponsored the concerts. They knew how to party, so naturally, Trudy, a vet's groupie was there. I spotted her from afar, dancing with a guy I knew from The Club. I was tempted to cut in, but it looked like they were really into each other. I found myself feeling a little jealous even though what we had was nothing more than a one night stand. Nonetheless, I had come away from it liking Trudy – she was a good spirit.

Being out in the sun and wind all day getting stoned, I became a little burned out. I needed to get out of the elements, so I went home and crashed. In the middle of the night someone came knocking on the door. I peeked out the window and saw a woman standing on the porch. I flicked on the porch light and saw, to my utter surprise that it was Cathy, the hostile hippie chick. "What the hell did she want this time of night...," I wondered, "...to get on my ass about Vietnam again?"

But she seemed sober so I opened the door. I could see that she was crying.

"What's up?" I asked.

"Can we talk?"

"If it's about Vietnam, no."

"I'm sorry to say it is about Vietnam, but I'm not here to harass you about it. My brother's been drafted and he's going there in the infantry. I'm afraid he'll be killed."

"Come in."

We sat at the kitchen table.

"I'm feeling terribly frustrated, Mick. I've been so outspoken against the war, and now my brother will be participating in it. Can you give me some reason to support it?"

"Sure, to stop the spread of Communism."

"What's so bad about Communism?"

"You've participated in the antiwar demonstrations here at SIU, right?"

"Of course."

"If you lived in a Communist country you wouldn't be allowed to. You'd be imprisoned or executed. In places like the Soviet Union and Red China dissidence is considered a crime. Stalin and Mao have murdered millions for it. So has Pol Pot in Cambodia."

In response to my argument, Cathy was silent for moment, then she reached across the table, held my hand and looked into my eyes, smiling.

"I've been going to AA and I'm working on Step 8 which says to make a list of all persons we have harmed, and become willing to make amends to them all, so I'd like to say I'm sorry, Mick, for giving you such a hard time on Halloween."

"I must admit it was hurtful, but that's in the past. We'll let bygones be bygones. So tell me, why did you decide to go to AA, at such a young age?"

"In a word, hangovers. I couldn't handle the hangovers."

"I know what you mean, maybe I should go someday, but I'm not ready yet. I enjoy the buzz too much, hangovers notwithstanding. Only problem is, my drinking has caused me to flunk out of school."

"What are you going to do now?"

"I'm working at a tree nursery to save enough money to go to Austin, Texas. Heard that's a hip place to be, and the winters are mild."

"I've heard the same thing."

"Wanna go get breakfast at Mary Lou's?" I asked. "I think she opens at 5. It's about that now."

"Yeah, I'm pretty hungry."

# CHAPTER 5

By August I had saved enough money to make the trip to Austin. Before I left, I went to the library where Cathy worked, to say goodbye.

"When are you leaving?" she asked.

"Tomorrow."

"Would you like to come to my place tonight for dinner?"

"That'd be great. What time?"

"Say around seven."

When I arrived, to my surprise, Cathy was drinking wine.

"I stopped going to AA," she sheepishly explained, as if she needed to. "But I'm not as out of control when I drink now. I'm more at peace than I used to be, especially regarding the war, since my brother is participating in it, and I've finally come to the conclusion, with a little help from you, that it's being fought for the freedom of the Vietnamese people."

"I wish I could say the same. With every passing day I've become more and more aware that it may be a lost cause."

"How so?"

"We're beginning to withdraw some of our troops. Eventually, I believe, we'll be turning the entire war over to the South Vietnamese. If we do I'm afraid they'll surely be defeated without us. That light at the end of the tunnel we hear so much about will be from North Vietnamese Army tanks invading the south."

"Well I hope my brother gets home before that happens."

Cathy poured a glass of wine for me, and she topped hers off, then she toasted to my trip to Austin and our friendship, and in the mellow glow of the candle light, as we ate, I secretly envisioned her as a potential lover, should we meet again someday.

# CHAPTER 6

It was a sunny Saturday afternoon when I left Carbondale. I drove down through Cairo at the southern tip of Illinois, and across the Mississippi River into the vast bottom lands of southeast Missouri. Shimmering heat waves rose from the road ahead, looking like pools of water on the pavement. Even the breeze blowing through the windows of my station wagon felt hot. I grew thirsty and stopped at an old gas station for a pop and directions to the next highway heading west into northern Arkansas. As I got into the hills the air cooled and the drive was pleasant with the road shaded here and there with trees. By and by I came to a lake that required a ferry crossing.

*"God's country,"* I said to myself, which made me laugh a little. Ever since Vietnam I had stopped believing in God. No benevolent creator would allow such a thing as war, I had decided, especially wars of religion like those being fought in the Middle East and in Northern Ireland. Yes, I had lost faith. Now I worshiped at an altar called a bar. This made me laugh, too. I wanted to find a bar soon. No road trip would be complete without a few beers. I'd find a bar or two in Eureka Springs, where I planned to spend the night, but I'd need to eat before I started drinking. I pulled over at a little hamburger stand a few miles from Eureka Springs to coat my stomach with grease, which I'd heard was good to do before one drank. I devoured a cheeseburger and fries.

Eureka Springs, I knew, was a tourist town built into the rocky hills and ravines of the Ozark Mountains. The natives called them mountains. For the Midwest they were. The streets wound around and up and down through the town, which consisted of old turn-of-the-century buildings housing restaurants and souvenir and antique shops. I parked at the bottom of a hill on a side street. This was where I'd sleep that night, in the back of the station wagon.

I walked around until sundown, looking in the windows of various stores, which appeared to cater mostly to antique hunters, until I came to a place that had a neon beer sign in the front window. Just what I was looking for. I walked in. It wasn't very busy, perhaps because it was still early. I sat on a stool at the bar and ordered a beer. While waiting, I looked up and saw above the back bar, a large mural of a wagon train heading west across the plains, where a herd of buffalo grazed. Appropriate for a place called Buffalo Bob's.

By the time I had started on my third beer, it had become dark outside, and the place was crowded and noisy. But the room quieted down when a young bearded man with long red hair like mine, sat on a stool and began to play a guitar and sing songs. I didn't recognize the tunes – the singer must have written them himself. His voice was strong and passionate, and he told good stories. One in particular caught my ear – a song about a Vietnam War veteran coming home.

"A Jet Lag War," was the title of the tune, and it contrasted previous wars, in which soldiers came home in ships that took several days, sometimes weeks, to traverse the oceans, with Vietnam soldiers who came home in jet airliners sometimes just one day removed from combat, and were expected to fit back into normal society, literally overnight. Some just couldn't readjust so quickly. It was uncanny how my story paralleled the musician's songs. The only difference was that the guy in the song turned to Jesus to help him get through his difficult times. That was something I didn't do any more because I was totally disillusioned with religion because of the war, and what my sisters and I went through as children, living with a maniacal, alcoholic mother. I had prayed for some relief from the chaos, but it never came, except briefly when our grandparents took us in. When mother took us back again, the chaos resumed.

The jet lag song was the only one with a religious theme; the others were about wanderlust and drinking, with which I identified closely. I had, after all, wandered into Arkansas, where I ended up drinking, which, as usual, made me uninhibited. I applauded the musician loudly whenever he finished a song. This attracted his attention of course, and when he took a break he came over to me and introduced himself.

"Name's Jeff," he smiled.

"Mick. What's happening, Jeff?"

"Everything, man. Where ya from?"

"Illinois, Carbondale," I replied.

"Carbondale, huh? I've been there. Hip little town."

"Are you from around here?" I asked.

"Tulsa. Originally Chicago though. Lots of people from Chicago here. Popular place to retire."

"But this is a younger crowd," I observed.

"Yeah, most come over from the university in Fayetteville. Do you smoke?" Jeff asked me out of the blue, in a low voice, almost whispering.

I grinned. "Not cigarettes."

"No, I mean, well, you know," Jeff said.

"Oh, okay, yeah, I do on occasion."

It was a habit I had picked up in 'Nam. Many GIs had. Pot was plentiful over there.

"Care to join me for a toke up the street before I start my next set?" Jeff asked.

"Okay."

I followed him outside. We went up the street – literally. It had a steep incline. We went into an alley about a half block away. The alley was short. It led to a cliff where dilapidated concrete stairs descended about 25 or 30 feet below. We stopped at the edge, and Jeff produced a joint. He lit it, took a hit, and passed it to me.

"So what d'ya do, Mick?"

"Nothing now. I was a student, but I flunked out. So tell me, Jeff, do you make a living playing your music?"

"Enough to pay the rent, with a little left over for food, and gas and this."

We passed the joint back and forth a couple of times, then Jeff smothered it with a thumb and index finger that he had wet with spit, and put it in a shirt pocket.

"Gotta get back to the gig, nice meet'n' ya, Mick."

"Yeah, same here."

The rest of the night became a little foggy, because I drank more until last call. Jeff had quit playing, and most of his audience had left. I was the last one to leave, but a few people were standing around outside. They were watching something going on down the street at the bottom of the hill.

"What's happening down there?" I asked.

"The cops are rounding up vagrants," somebody said.

"You live around here?' one of the bystanders inquired.

"No."

"Then you better make yourself scarce if you don't have a place to stay, or they'll haul your ass off to jail."

I had planned on sleeping in my station wagon. To get there I'd have to pass the police. I started down the hill, but before I got very far they came up to me and asked where I lived. I said Illinois.

I decided instantly that I would not go to jail just for being on the street, after all there was no martial law in effect. They asked to see my driver's license. As soon as they handed it back, I had decided to take off for the alley up the street, where Jeff and I had been smoking. The very second my license touched my finger tips I started running. It was a difficult run up such a steep incline. The cops were older, they wouldn't be able to catch me. I ducked into the alley, but I was going so fast I wasn't able negotiate the stairs step-by-step, so I leapt off the cliff and quickly realized it was further to the ground than I had anticipated. I began to tumble forward, and landed face first in thick spongy underbrush. I bounced back up and dashed through a dense stand of trees, when suddenly the ground beneath me gave way. It wasn't ground after all, but old chicken wire overgrown with vines that stretched across a deep creek. I landed on my buttocks and back hard on round rocks submerged in shallow water. I lay just as I landed trying to be still, stifling my heavy breathing and listening for the police.

There was an opening above me in the chicken wire through which I had fallen, but much of it, still covered with vegetation, had remained intact, keeping me fairly well camouflaged. I heard rustling in the underbrush, but no voices. After a while the rustling ceased; I continued to lie perfectly still.

They could be standing nearby, listening quietly for me to make some noise – if they thought I hadn't run all the way through the woods.

The water began to feel cold on my back, rump and legs, and my sweaty face stung from the scratches the broken chicken wire had made. One of my legs, which was folded underneath me when I landed in the stream on my back, began to cramp. I stretched it out slowly, to relieve the pain, and soon, woozy from the ordeal, I passed out.

When the sun came up in the morning, I felt that it was safe to move. I stood up slowly. Every muscle in my body was stiff, but I was able to climb out of the creek bed on the chicken wire, and I made a beeline to where I had parked my car. It was gone. The cops had probably run the Illinois plates and found that the car belonged to me, remembering my name from the Illinois driver's license. They had it towed after I ran from them, so I was forced to turn myself in to get it back.

At the station one of the cops greeted me.

"I ain't tryin' to be a smart Alec or nothin', son, but after that fall you took last night, you better turn to Jesus!"

After I got the car back, which entailed paying a towing and storage fee, I continued on to Austin. While driving I thought about what the cop had said about turning to Jesus. There was no doubt that I had lucked out escaping serious injury taking that fall, but I doubted whether it was because of divine intervention. I was more inclined to think that it was just a matter of luck, but of course I really didn't know for sure. It could have been luck bestowed on me by Jesus, I supposed. For me to even consider such a possibility was a step in the right direction toward restoring my faith. I wanted so much to have faith in something.

# CHAPTER 7

It was a long drive to Austin and I drove straight through, stopping only for gas and food, and visits to the john. When I arrived on a Monday afternoon I checked into a motel and caught up on some sleep. Tuesday morning, feeling well-rested I drove around to familiarize myself with the town. It was bigger than I expected, being the state capital and home of the University of Texas. Looming above the campus was the infamous Texas Tower, from which Charles Whitman gunned down several people a few years earlier.

Around noon I stopped at a taco stand downtown for lunch. There was a newspaper machine nearby. I bought a paper and sat on a bench overlooking the Colorado River to eat while I scanned the classifieds hoping to find a place to rent right away. It would be too expensive to stay in a motel night after night.

There was a relatively cheap furnished efficiency being advertised by a bank. It was located in a section of south Austin called Travis Heights. I called the number and arranged to meet the bank's property manager that afternoon at the apartment. It was a block from a nice little linear park with a rocky stream running through it. A privacy fence enclosed a yard at the back of a house with a larger apartment at its front.

Pleased with the place, I paid two months rent in advance, assuring that I'd have a roof over my head until I could find a job. This left me with barely enough money to buy food, gas, and a cheap six-pack or two now and then.

Consulting the newspaper I saw that landscaping jobs were plentiful in Austin, because it was a semi-tropical city with a year-round growing season. It didn't take long to get hired because I was experienced in that line of work. Most of the men I worked with were Mexican-Americans. They worked hard and said very little except to each other, in Spanish, which left me feeling somewhat alienated. One of them, a guy named Ramon, who was the foreman of the crew I worked on, was courteous enough to speak to me in English. We gradually became friends, and occasionally had a beer or two after work on Saturday nights, at a Mexican bar on East 6th Street. A band played there and they sounded remarkably similar to a polka band, featuring an accordion. After getting primed on Coronas, Ramon danced to the music with a pretty little lady named Maria who was also a regular there.

She had a younger sister, Bonita, to whom they introduced me, and we enjoyed sitting at the table drinking while watching Ramon and Maria dance. Between musical numbers they returned to the table and we all conversed in both English and Spanish. Ramon and Bonita interpreted for me and Maria who spoke only Spanish . Bonita spoke primarily in English, her accent made her speech sound delightfully exotic.

Like so many Mexican women she had a beautiful brown face framed in shiny black hair. She had a well-proportioned, busty body with strong looking shoulders, arms and legs that were usually visible because she wore tank tops and shorts. I got the impression she was an athlete of some kind.

The four of us got along famously, laughing and joking in two languages, but because I was especially attracted to Bonita, I wanted to relate to her one-on-one, so I invited her to a concert with me at a popular venue called the Armadillo World Headquarters. Despite the loud music, we were able to carry on a conversation. It was a little stiff at first because this was the first time we were alone together, but it loosened up after a drink or two.

"I'm assuming you don't have a girlfriend or wife, Mick. I think that is something we should establish early on."

"Understood. I'm clean. I'm assuming the same thing about you."

"Si."

"Then I guess we can proceed uninhibited."

"So tell me, Mick, just how uninhibited are you?"

"In what sense?"

"Sexually."

I was taken aback by the directness of her answer.

"I don't think I'm any more inhibited in that respect than normal," I said.

"Have you ever cross dressed.," she asked. "I mean with your pretty long hair, feminine features and slender legs (I was wearing shorts) you could pass as a woman if you wore the right clothes."

As a macho man I wasn't comfortable with being likened to a woman, or Bonita suggesting that I dress like one, so I shifted the focus of the conversation away from me and onto her.

"No offense, Bonita, but you have certain masculine qualities, and I mean that as a compliment – you look athletic. So, have you ever cross dressed?"

"On Halloween. My greatest fantasy is cross dressing with a man, but I've never met one who was willing. Would you be? Halloween is coming up. You'd make a great Ann Margaret with your long reddish hair."

"And who would you be?"

"Elvis. With my dark features I'd be a natural. Those two were rumored to be lovers, you know."

I wondered if that was what all of this was leading up to – making love while cross dressed. That wasn't in my book of desirable fantasies. Was it in hers?

"We could buy your clothes at a thrift store. I'm a hair stylist so I could make your hair look like Ann's. Oh, and you'd have to get used to wearing high heels – we'd be bar hopping."

"Couldn't I just wear flats?" The very nature of the question seemed to indicate that I was at least contemplating Bonita's proposal that I cross dress with her.

"Ann Margaret never wore flats in her life. Her baby shoes were stilettos. Besides, flats aren't very sexy. Nor are hairy legs – you'd have to shave."

"This is beginning to sound like The Rocky Horror Picture Show."

"Exactly. That's how we'd start the evening off. There's an early showing on Halloween at a theater near campus, then we'd go downtown."

Bonita was quite presumptuous about my participation in her kinky fantasy. I just couldn't picture myself in drag. And I sure as hell didn't want to shave my legs or wear high heels. And there was no way I could make out with a woman who was dressed like Elvis Presley, so I put an end to the conversation by telling her she would have to find somebody else, and that put an end to our evening together.

A couple of nights later I dreamt about being dressed like Ann Margaret, which was terribly disturbing because it turned out to be a wet dream. Had Bonita's strange fantasy become mine? Was the thought of dressing like a woman a turn-on?

Feeling a little insecure about my masculinity now, I tested the notion hoping to put such a notion to rest. I went to a thrift store, bought a dress and heels and tried them on at home. I discovered that it wasn't a turn-on after all, but I was intrigued by my ability to temporarily transition from one sex to another simply by changing clothes.

I was curious as to whether I could pull it off in public. The next time I met with Ramon, Maria and Bonita for drinks, I agreed to go along with Bonita's Halloween masquerade, just for the hell of it. So, as the appointed hour neared I shaved my legs and practiced walking in high heels. Halloween afternoon Bonita came to my apartment, did my hair and applied makeup. I put on the stockings and garter belt she provided, donned the dress I had bought, and we went off into the night – first to the Rocky Horror Picture Show, then bar hopping on 6th Street. We started at the venerable Driscol Hotel where we sat on the veranda and drank, and Bonita was right when she predicted that I'd pass, for the waitress addressed me as ma'am and her as sir, although we did garner a second look or two. I didn't talk much because my voice was too deep for a woman's, but Bonita's was relatively deep like Elvis's was, so she ordered the drinks.

Emboldened by the alcohol, we continued bar hopping down the street. As we walked I got a dose of what it was like to be gawked at, and in one case whistled at by a man because apparently to him, I looked like an attractive woman. But when we passed under a street light it became apparent that I wasn't a woman, and the man yelled "faggot!" We ducked into the nearest dimly-lit bar. It was in this bar that I was approached by a drunk man who blubbered sweet nothings in my ear while moving his hand up under my dress. When he discovered that I wasn't a woman after all, he took at roundhouse swing at me, which I ducked. I grabbed Bonita, pulled her out the door, and we ran down the street. Not used to running in high heels, I twisted my ankle and fell flat on my face. I tried to get up but I couldn't put any weight on my foot. Bonita hailed a taxi and directed the driver to take me to a hospital.

Sitting under the bright light of the emergency room in drag I became extremely self-conscious and wanted to crawl under the chair and hide. Despite having drunk quite a bit of alcohol I was sober now and fully felt the pain in my ankle. It had swollen as big as a baseball. Bonita tried to comfort me by lifting my leg onto her lap to keep the ankle elevated, but it continued to throb as if it were being pounded with a hammer. I suspected it was broken.

Finally I was called in for x-rays, and they revealed that the ankle was indeed broken. It was put in a cast and I was given crutches to help me walk, then they sent me on my way. We took a taxi back to where Bonita had parked her car, and she drove me home. Her kinky fantasy to get it on with me dressed as a woman was never fulfilled.

Because of the broken ankle I was no longer able to work as a landscaper. I hadn't anticipated the injury, of course, so I hadn't saved any money: I had lived from paycheck to paycheck. By next payday, I would be broke.

I had a box of macaroni and cheese, two cans of tuna in the cabinet, a jar of pickles and three beers in the fridge, and a half a tank of gas.

When all of that was gone, I hobbled around the neighborhood with plastic bags tied to my crutches picking up pecans that had fallen from the trees. As a last resort, I put a "For Sale" sign on my car. It sold fast and I was able to catch up on rent with enough money left over to buy a ticket on the train, the Texas Eagle running from San Antonio through Austin to Chicago with a stop in Springfield, Illinois, my home town. I wouldn't be going back to Carbondale because I was no longer a student.

By the time I got back to Springfield I was starving and out of money. To eat I went to St. John's Breadline. I had no idea where I'd sleep that night. I had lost touch with friends and I was too proud to ask my sisters for help.

Wandering around, I discovered a homeless shelter, but it was filled to capacity, so I was turned out onto the street. The weather was cold – I needed to find a warm place to sleep, like a church. I knew that some left their doors unlocked all night, which I discovered was the case with the First Presbyterian Church, where Abe Lincoln and his family had worshiped, according to a plaque on the big red double doors.

It was ironic that a man resentful toward religion would depend on a church for food and shelter. That dependency would continue for as long as I was on crutches and unable to work.

After about two weeks I went to a free clinic to have my ankle checked out, and they determined it was time to remove the cast. I immediately searched for work, but it was winter there were no landscaping jobs so I took a job tending bar and slinging pizzas at a popular sports tavern called DiLello's Tap. After a week of bartending I was able to rent a room upstairs, and I was back to living above a tavern again as I had when I was in high school. At least it gave me a mailing address. I soon got a letter from the Veteran's Administration telling me that I had two years of eligibility left on my GI Bill and I needed to enroll in a college within the next six months or I would forfeit it. So I visited a relatively new local university (Sangamon State) to see if the credits I had earned at Southern Illinois University were transferable. Some were, so I enrolled.

Sangamon State was considered to be an innovative educational institution at which students, faculty and staff interacted like one big happy family in providing a unique academic experience.

Because I had majored in radio and television production at SIU and the Armed Forces Journalism School in the Air Force, I continued with that curriculum at SSU. I became a disc jockey on the campus radio station, earning work/study credits toward a degree.

In the meantime I continued tending bar at DiLello's which earned me enough money to move out of the room upstairs and into a one-bedroom apartment, with enough left over to buy a clunker to get me back and forth between work, school and home.

While tending bar, I met a woman who had heard me on the radio. She recognized my voice and said I sounded like Clint Eastwood in the haunting movie *Play Misty For Me.* And like the woman in the movie played by Jessica Lang, she began to call me at the station every night to tell me how much she enjoyed listening to me, which I didn't mind so much since my ego enjoyed the positive feedback.

One Friday night after my shift, she invited me to meet her for a drink at a downtown bar. Her request seemed reasonable enough, so I obliged. The woman was a little chubby, but she had a nice face that was highlighted by pretty hazel eyes. The conversation started off normally, but with each drink she became increasingly hostile.

"Glad you came," she said. "Most radio guys are too stuck up to socialize with their listeners. The guy who was on before you wouldn't give me the time of day when I called. At least you take my calls, even though you sometimes sound a little put off. I'm only trying to be your friend. It's kind of lonely out here, but you probably don't know what that feels like because you're a celebrity."

"Oh, I don't think of myself as being a celebrity. I just play music. The musicians are the celebrities."

"You don't have to play Mr. Humble with me. I know you think you're special, I can hear it in your voice. May I ask you a personal question, do you smoke pot?"

"On occasion."

"I've got some really good shit. Wanna go to my car and try some?"

"Well, yeah, I guess."

When we got to her car she loaded a pipe with what I thought was pot and handed it to me, then she lit it with a lighter. After drawing a few good puffs I handed it back to her. She declined, which I thought was peculiar because she had provided the pot.

I didn't think much more about it, though, and I continued to puff on the pipe, trying to get high, but never did. It only made me sick to my stomach, so I excused myself, went to my car and drove home.

The next afternoon my entire face began to itch, and by the following morning my eyes and nostrils were swollen shut and oozing with pus, and my lips were puffed up and itching. I went to a doctor. He asked me if I had been standing near a yard waste fire.

"It appears as if you've been exposed to poison ivy smoke."

Then it hit me. The so-called pot I had smoked from the pipe of the woman I had met for drinks was actually poison ivy. No wonder she didn't partake. I'd been set up by the sadistic bitch. She had it in for disc jockeys.

Monday night I got a call from a woman requesting the song *Poison Ivy* by the Coasters. She ended the call by laughing madly.

# CHAPTER 8

Besides my internship at the radio station to fulfill the requirements for a major in Communications, I took a Beat Literature course to earn enough credits for a minor in English. It was conducted in the home of the instructor Randy Randazzo. Randazzo had managed to persuade Lawrence Ferlinghetti, the Beat poet, to come to Springfield from San Francisco for a lecture at the university, followed by a spaghetti dinner at Randy's house for the poet and the class.

When I met the affable poet, he extended an open invitation for me to visit his City Lights Book Store in San Francisco. When the spring semester ended, I took him up on it. In the spirit of the famous Beat author Jack Kerouac's classic *On the Road,* I decided to hitchhike to the City by the Bay, because I couldn't depend on my clunker of a car to get me out to the west coast and back. I couldn't afford to fly and I didn't like traveling on buses and trains that stopped frequently. And if I spent most of my money on transportation getting there and back I wouldn't have enough money to rent a place in San Francisco for the summer. Hitchhiking was the frugal thing to do.

Consulting an atlas, I determined that the best way to go would be down Interstate 55 from Springfield to St. Louis, west to Denver on I-70 and north to Cheyenne on I-25, where I'd catch I-80 to San Francisco.

On a sunny, late spring afternoon, I left, with a backpack and sleeping bag in tow.

I got rides to St. Louis with a variety of people who were apparently adventurous too, or they wouldn't have stopped for a long-haired stranger like me.

I was surprised that one of them was with a middle-aged woman with a little black poodle sitting on her lap. The dog growled when I got in.

"Shhh, Fritzy," the woman said.

He sniffed at my arm, and decided I was okay. At least that's what the wagging tail seemed to indicate.

"I'm going to St. Louis," she said. "I hope that'll help."

"Sure will. Thanks."

"Is St. Louis your destination?" she asked.

"No. I'm on my way to San Francisco, but I'm going to Denver first, on I-70."

"Oh, I can get you to 70 just west of St. Louis. I live out that way.

"My grandson lives in California, San Jose. He's an attorney. Hah, he has a pony tail too." She chuckled. "I can't imagine a lawyer with a pony tail, but he does all right. They're pretty liberal out there. I'm not as liberal as he is. It doesn't run in the family," she volunteered. "My guess is that you're a liberal."

"I am now, but I didn't used to be."

"What changed you?"

"The war."

"Don't tell me you're one of those protesters."

"No. I'm too laid back for that. I oppose the war passively."

"Like in passive resistance?"

"I guess you could say that."

"Does that mean you're a draft dodger, like that boxer Cassius Clay was?"

"No. I got drafted."

"Did you have to go to Vietnam?"

"Yeah. That's why I'm opposed to the war. I experienced it first hand."

"You have a right to your opinion. But I'm in support of the war if it'll stop the spread of Communism."

"That should be left up to the South Vietnamese people to decide, without interference from us," I said.

The woman smiled. "In that case I guess we'll just have to agree to disagree. Right Fritzy?"

The dog barked.

As we crossed the Mississippi River I looked down at the brown water moving swiftly under the bridge as we crossed into St. Louis. I was reminded of the Lewis and Clark expedition, initiating the United States's westward expansion beyond this great river, all the way to the Pacific Ocean. The sleek, stainless steel Gateway Arch gleaming high in the sky ahead symbolized this.

After a few more miles the woman informed me that her exit was coming up. "When I let you out, just walk over to the ramp across the way. It merges back onto the interstate."

The traffic was heavy and moving fast. One big rig after another blew past. If someone had slowed down to stop they'd surely have been rear ended. That didn't deter a guy in a jalopy from coming to a sudden stop on the shoulder about 20 yards down the road. I ran after him and hopped in.

"Toss your stuff in the back," he said. "Where ya headed?"

"Eventually, San Francisco."

"I can take you as far as Kansas City."

I noticed he was drinking a can of beer. Part of a six-pack sat on the seat between us.

"Want one? They're still cold."

"Sure. I'm pretty thirsty. Kind of hot today. Thanks. You live in Kansas City?'

"No. I'm just going there for a going away party for a friend of mine who joined the Navy. Gonna send him off with a rip-roaring hangover. I'll have one too."

He took another swig of beer, and so did I.

He was driving pretty fast, and weaving in and out of traffic. I was beginning to wish I hadn't gotten this ride.

"Goin' to San Francisco, huh? That's where my buddy Jake ships out from – to Vietnam. Hear it's pretty bad over there."

"Yeah," I concurred.

"You been there?" the guy asked.

"Yeah."

"Hey, why don't you come to the party? You can fill Jake in on what to expect over there. It's going to be dark pretty soon, you could crash on his couch and take off again in the morning when it's light out."

I didn't like the thought of hitchhiking at night, and the beers I'd drunk had put me in a partying mood, so I took the guy up on his invitation.

When we arrived at the party, we had finished the six pack, but a keg was waiting -- along with Jake, and six other people. Two were young women who looked like they were barely old enough to drink. In fact, everyone looked like that, but, boy, could they drink! In addition to the beer, they were drinking from a big bowl of red punch into which I saw someone pour a bottle of some kind of clear booze.

Ricky – the guy who had picked me up, introduced me to Jake, and he told him I was a Vietnam veteran.

"Know anything about the Mekong Delta?" he asked. "That's where I'm going. I'll be with the Riverines."

I knew that it was dangerous down there, especially for the Riverines, but I didn't want to alarm Jake, so I simply said, "It's hot."

"Like Kitty here?" Jake wrapped an arm around one of the women and squeezed her.

I had to admit, she was nice looking – a full-figured blond with big blue eyes like Cathy Riggins.

"Kitty, meet Mick."

"Hi, Mick. Ricky told me you're going to San Francisco. Lucky you. I'd love to go there someday."

"Go with him," Jake said. "I'm sure he wouldn't mind. You'd get rides pretty fast."

We chuckled, knowing Jake was only kidding. But his light-hearted suggestion opened the door for more serious conversation between Kitty and me. She asked me if I had a girlfriend.

"No."

"I don't have a boyfriend, in case you thought it was Jake. We're just friends."

Apparently a drunk and slobbering Jake didn't see it that way. He pawed Kitty while she tried to talk to me, so I took her hand and we went outside to the back porch for a refreshing breath of night air. It was a little cool, so I draped my denim jacket around Kitty's shoulders and she snuggled up to me. We embraced and kissed. We stayed on the porch for quite a while until it got too chilly. When we went back inside, the party had fizzled out. Jake had crashed in his bedroom, Ricky was passed out in a recliner, and the others were gone.

Kitty and I lay on the couch and continued to make out, but she was drunk from the potent punch, and she soon fell asleep in my arms. Before long I did the same. When I woke up at the crack of dawn, Kitty was gone. On my chest was a note: "Thanks for rescuing me from my 'friend' Jake."

I grabbed my backpack and sleeping bag and headed out. Jake's apartment wasn't far from the interstate, so it wasn't long before I was at it again with my thumb out.

As in St. Louis, the Kansas City traffic was heavy and fast-moving. I walked for a couple of miles, until I came to a truck stop, where I had a bite to eat. A chubby guy with long, dark sideburns and a mustache, who was sitting at one of the tables, motioned for me to come over to him.

"I saw you hitchhiking a ways back, but I couldn't stop. If you'll wait till I finish my breakfast I'll give you a ride. I'm going to Denver. Will that help?"

"Sure will."

It was a bouncy ride. The shocks in that 18-wheeler weren't very effective at absorbing the numerous bumps on the road, but it beat standing on the side of the road being buffeted by the violent draft from passing trucks that blew grit in my eyes.

Apart from the bouncing, I enjoyed riding up high with a panoramic view of the green Kansas plains rolling endlessly into the treeless blue horizon. The plains were austere compared to the wooded hills of Missouri through which I'd traveled the day before.

The driver's personality was just as austere. He didn't speak for miles, and not until I spoke to him.

"How long have you been a truck driver?" I asked.

"Counting convoy duty in Vietnam -- four years."

"I'm a 'Nam vet too."

"Oh yeah? What did you do there?"

"I was a combat correspondent for Armed Forces Radio."

"A reporter, huh?"

He sounded a little put off by the revelation.

"Civilian or military?" he asked.

"Military."

"Then you probably told the truth unlike those civilian assholes."

"For the most part. There were a few things we weren't allowed to say."

"Like what?"

"In '67 we wouldn't admit that there were North Vietnamese soldiers in such great numbers in the south, or that we used napalm, because it was considered inhumane."

"What a joke." He laughed. "We were constantly being ambushed by the North Vietnamese in '67, and the Air Force used napalm to fend them off."

The driver had gone from taciturn to outspoken.

"That's the trouble with this war. The press has bamboozled the American people. I'll give you another example. The Tet Offensive of '68 was a devastating defeat for the Viet Cong, yet Walter Cronkite made it out to be a victory for them. He said the war had become a stalemate, even though we kicked the enemy's ass. Hell, LBJ decided not to run for a second term because of what Cronkite said. No newsman should have that much power. So here we are in 1972 and we're about to pull out of the war before the job gets done,"

We rode along in silence again, mile after mile through Kansas and the high plains of eastern Colorado, and gradually, in the hazy distance, the Rocky Mountains and Denver's skyline appeared.

The sun was setting behind the mountains, which cast their purple-gray shadows over the city, but there was still plenty of time left in the day for me to catch a ride north to Cheyenne before dark. I'd told the driver that was where I'd be going, so, as we approached Denver, he let me out on a clover leaf that circled into I-25.

By the time I got to Cheyenne via piecemeal rides, it had gotten dark, so I checked into a cheap motel to get a warm shower and a good night's rest.

I slept fairly well and got an early start going west on I-80. The weather was warm for Wyoming in the spring. Because of the altitude, the air was thinner than I was accustomed to, and I got winded walking as I hitchhiked. I plopped down on my backpack and nonchalantly stuck my thumb out, appearing indifferent, I'm sure, as to whether I got a ride or not. Sometimes when you don't try as hard, things come your way, and they did when two teenagers in a pickup truck stopped and motioned for me to ride in the back. It was now late afternoon, and it was chilly as the wind blew over me. I was relieved to get out of the wind when they stopped at a roadhouse on a secondary highway at the edge of the Medicine Bow National Forest, according to a sign I saw.

To my puzzlement, after I got out of the truck, they sped away, laughing wildly. What was so damn funny, I wondered, about dropping me off in the middle of nowhere? I soon found out. When I entered the establishment, I saw that it was a cowboy hangout. Cowboys didn't take kindly to long hairs with pony tails, at least the male kind, judging from the looks of animosity I received.

Those mischievous boys knew what they were getting me into.

The bartender didn't seem too enthusiastic about my presence either. He asked me, in an unfriendly tone, what I wanted.

"Whatever's on tap," I said.

He slid a beer in front of me and snatched up my money without saying thanks. The others in the bar stared at me, and I drank the beer as fast as I could. I wanted to get out of the place quickly. I was reminded of the Lynyrd Skynyrd song about the long hair who happened into a red neck roadhouse, which pleaded: *"Give me three steps mister, give me three steps for the door, and you won't see me no more."*

After I left, I started walking in the direction from which I thought I had come, but after about two miles I realized I was going the wrong way, and was heading toward the forest. It was almost nightfall and there was no traffic going either way, so I decided to bed down in the forest, in the sleeping bag I had with me.

The forest floor was soft with fallen pine needles, and quite comfortable. I was warm enough in the sleeping bag, despite the chilly air, laden with the soothing scent of pine. The stark silence, save for the faint whispering of a breeze in the trees, was a welcome relief from the noisy interstates I'd been on for the last two days. Or was it three? Damn, I was losing track of time, and the number of miles I had gone, with many more to go before I reached San Francisco, and Ferlinghetti's City Lights Book Store.

In the morning, after a peaceful night's sleep, I began what I thought would be about a five mile trek back to I-80. There was almost no traffic -- not surprising for a dead end road -- so I ended up walking all the way back to the interstate. Luckily, there was a Stuckey's restaurant there. I had a big breakfast becasuse I hadn't eaten for a while. Then I was on my way again. After getting a series of relatively short rides, then one long one with a rancher hauling horses, I reached Utah before a VW bus painted with peace signs and flowers, with New York plates and four hippies inside, pulled over.

"Where ya going?" one of them asked through an open window.

"San Francisco."

"You're in luck. We're going there too. Climb in."

They looked like a rock band on tour. One of the women strummed a guitar and the other one thumped and jingled a tambourine. The inside of the van smelled like marijuana. A joint was going around. They assumed, I guess, that because I had long hair, I would gladly partake. They were right. When the joint came around to me I took a hit and passed it on. Around it went, and before long I was delightfully stoned, and some of the words to Scott McKenzie's hit song came to mind: *"If you're going to San Francisco be sure to wear some flowers in your hair."* And these women did wear flowers in their hair. I asked the woman that the others called Abigail why they were going to San Francisco.

"For the Summer of Love reunion in June," she said.

I had been in Vietnam when it happened, but I'd read about in the *Pacific Stars and Stripes* newspaper. It was a rousing rockfest featuring Jefferson Airplane, the Grateful Dead, the Who, the Doors, Janis Joplin and Jimi Hendrix, to name just a few.

"How about you?" Abigail asked.

"To visit Lawrence Ferlinghetti at his City Lights Book Store."

"Far out!" she exclaimed.

One of the men asked me if I was a poet too.

"Sort of. I've written a few poems."

"Far out," was his response also.

Far out, for sure. I had become totally stoned out of my mind. Too stoned to talk much more. Apparently the others were, too, and we rode along in silence for quite a while.

It was another three-joint stretch across Utah and around Salt Lake City, and eventually into Nevada. We drove all night and then some. They switched drivers when we stopped for gas and bought Twinkies and Fritos to take care of the munchies.

By morning we were driving through Reno and into the Sierra Mountains of California. We took a side trip to Lake Tahoe, and went for a swim in a secluded cove. We weren't the least bit inhibited about seeing each other naked, even though we were total strangers. The cold mountain water was refreshing after riding in a stuffy van for so many miles.

Reinvigorated after the swim, we embarked on the last leg of the journey around Sacramento and to San Francisco through Oakland and across the Bay Bridge. As we crossed the bridge, the towering Transamerica Pyramid Building, Coit Tower and the magnificent Golden Gate Bridge came into view.

"We're going straight into Haight-Ashbury," Peter, the driver, informed me. "We'll park in Golden Gate Park and try to get by with sleeping in the bus there tonight. It'll be too cramped in here for five, so I'd suggest that you find some place else to crash," he said matter-of-factly.

"Okay. Well then, thanks for the ride. So long."

They let me out at Haight and Market Streets and I walked around searching for a room to rent for the night. Haight-Ashbury didn't look like the vibrant flower power enclave I expected to see. It was 1972 -- the hippies had become burned out street people wandering about aimlessly while presumably bumming money to support their drug habits.

I was reluctant to stay in the area, but nightfall was fast approaching, and I needed to find a place to sleep. I went into a head shop and asked the clerk if he knew of any rooms to rent nearby.

"Yeah. Down the street – the Wayfarer Hotel. I think it costs about 30 bucks a night. But be warned, its more like a roach hotel," he said.

That was okay by me, for the time being anyway, as long as I had a bed to lie on.

A few blocks down, I saw the Wayfarer. It was easily identifiable by a flickering blue neon sign on the front of the building. I entered the small, musty-smelling lobby, where a seedy old man snored in a soiled, stuffed chair. I tapped on the bell next to a registration book on the front desk. He awoke with a start, and went behind the desk, grumbling. He asked gruffly if I wanted a room.

"Yeah."

"Thirty-five dollars for one night," he said. "No cooking or alcohol. Checkout at 11 a.m."

I gave him the money.

"You'll be in room 210. There's a bathroom at the end of the hall with a tub. Towels in the room."

I immediately took a bath, returned to my room, and lay down to sleep, but the flickering neon sign outside my window kept me a awake for a while. Eventually it began to have a hypnotic effect, and lulled me to sleep. In the morning I woke up in time to check out by eleven, and I asked the guy who was now on duty how to get to the North Beach area, where the City Lights Book Store was.

"Get on the Masonic Avenue bus going north, then transfer onto the Washington Street bus that goes east to Columbus Avenue. It'll stop at the Transamerica building. City Lights is about six blocks northwest of there on Columbus. It's a long ride."

When I finally reached Columbus Avenue, I got off the bus and walked the few blocks to the book store. On the way I stopped at a Cantonese restaurant for a delicious duck dinner (nobody does duck like the Chinese), then I went on to the book store, where I hoped to meet Ferlinghetti. If he was there, perhaps he'd remember me from his visit to Springfield.

In the store, a few people browsed among the many book shelves. It was quiet, except for the faint sound of jazz playing on a radio, or stereo. The place smelled a little musty, as used book stores do, even though the store sold new books, too.

Before long, I spotted Ferlinghetti – a man with a lean, angular face ands a graying goatee -- at the back shelving books. I approached him and told him that I was in Randy Randazzo's Beat lit class at Sangamon State in Springfield.

"Oh, wow! I didn't expect to see anyone from there all the way out here. What brings you to San Francisco?"

"You."

"Me?"

"Yeah. I'm planning to write a paper on the Beats, and I wanted to pick your brain on the movement's origin, and where it's at now."

"Well, you've come to the right place. Come to my office. We'll talk there."

His office was a cubby hole at the back of the store. It contained a couple of chairs, a desk and an electric typewriter with a half-typed sheet of paper in it. The desk was strewn with typewritten papers marked up with a pencil, evidence that he might have been working on a writing project. There was a coffee maker on a little table in the corner. He offered me a cup.

"Cream, sugar?" he asked.

"Black. Thanks."

He poured one for himself too, and sat at the desk.

"In answer to your question about what's happening with the Beat movement now – it's still barely alive, thanks to cats like Randazzo who teach it at the universities and colleges, and some high schools.

"As far as its origins, well, it goes all the way back to the early to mid-'40s in New York City and a group of up-and-coming writers at Columbia University. The group, which included Jack Kerouac, Allen Ginsberg, William Burroughs, Neal Cassady and myself, walked to the beat of a different drum – if you will – experimenting with alternative lifestyles, including certain drugs that we believed would enhance our writing. We were the original counter-culture. Eventually, with the popularity of Jack's *On the Road*, the Beat movement came to San Francisco, where it eventually became the hippie movement, which went nationwide, even to small towns in mid-America. But it, too, is beginning to die out. Have you been to Haight-Ashbury?"

"Yes. Yesterday."

"Then you may have noticed that the flowers have become a little wilted, except for the poppies. Heroin use is flourishing there, between sharing both needles and multiple sex partners, so is venereal disease. Good place to stay away from. North Beach is where it's at."

"So I've heard. I'd like to find a place to live around here for the summer."

"Consult the classifieds in the Chronicle," Ferlinghetti suggested.    "You can use my phone."

He left me alone in his office to look through the newspaper he'd handed me. I found an ad for an efficiency apartment on Columbus for $300 a month – very reasonable for this expensive city. I called the number to set up a meeting with the landlord, who sounded like an effeminate man. When we met, his physique was nothing like feminin. He was about 6'4" with a muscular build, enhanced by the tank top he wore. With his thick black mustache and hair, square chin and jaw, toothy smile and prominent dark eyes, he resembled Tom Selleck, but when he opened his mouth he sounded more like Farrah Fawcett.

"Follow me, I'll show you the apartment."

We went through an iron gate and onto a brick walk alongside the stucco building into a small courtyard at the back. He unlocked the door of the apartment, and we stepped inside. It had an Oriental motif with bamboo furniture. A large watercolor of a misty mountain scene hung on one of the walls. Another wall contained a Murphy bed. A bamboo curtain partitioned the room from a small kitchen. There was a small bathroom with a shower. It was a bright and airy little place, and I immediately agreed to rent it.

The courtyard was an unexpected feature I greatly appreciated, considering the reasonable rent and popular neighborhood. It was enclosed by tall, bushy arborvitae that made it very secluded. It would be a good place to smoke a joint now and then, if I ever scored some pot – which would surely be plentiful in this city. First I'd have to meet someone I could trust enough to make a deal with, that would require my socializing in a bar or café. I considered asking Ferlinghetti, but I hesitated making that kind of demand so early in our friendship. I didn't know if the man still smoked pot at his age.

There were many bars and cafes in North Beach and neighboring Chinatown. One bar in particular that I began to frequent was the Vesuvio on Columbus, across Jack Kerouac Alley from City Lights – a mere block from my apartment -- where the beatniks of old, sporting goatees and black berets, mingled with new age hippies in tie-dye to live their closely-similar Bohemian lifestyles. The walls were adorned with literary memorabilia. I noticed there was a signed black and white photo of Ferlinghetti and Ginsberg.

I got a beer at the bar and went up to the balcony, from which I had a good view of the happenings below. It was a Friday night, and the place was packed. When it was time to go down for another beer, I had to squeeze my way to the bar. I didn't mind though, because there were plenty of women doing the same, resulting in some close body contact, and some face-to-face encounters and conversations.

I had a friendly talk with a woman -- a red head, like me – whose breath was ripe with wine, and she smelled of weed. The alcohol I had consumed, emboldened me to inquire where I might find some of what she had apparently been smoking.

"I've got a joint in my purse," she admitted, aware that in San Francisco she probably wouldn't get busted for such a small amount, if I happened to be a narc.

"We can smoke it in the alley if you'd like," she proposed.

"Yes, I would like. But we don't have to do it in the alley. We can go to my place. It's just a block away."

"Okay," she said without hesitation.

We put our empty glasses down, and left the bar. Outside, away from the crowd, and the artificial courage of alcohol, we suddenly found ourselves in the sobering situation of two strangers trying to relate. We engaged in awkward small talk on the way to my place.

"I'm Mary Jane."

She looked as plain as her name, with straight, dish water blond hair, thin lips and beady brown eyes.

"Mick."

"Are you from San Francisco, Mick?"

"No. Illinois. And you?"

"Stockton originally, but I've lived here for ten years."

Then she popped the obligatory question that was so popular to ask among new age hipsters who were into astrology, like Trudy the townie had done in Carbondale when I lived there a couple of years before in 1971.

"What's your sign?"

"Scorpio."

"Far out. Me too."

When we arrived at my apartment we sat on the bench in the courtyard and lit the joint. We said nothing until we got off, and Mary Jane launched into a breathless diatribe about how cool it was for two Scorpios to meet by chance, "....a cosmic coincidence" she called it, "which Scorpes are known to experience on a regular basis because of our psychic powers. As lofty a characteristic as that is, we're also known to getting down and dirty. Each sign is related to a body part, and for us it's the genitals. We are the sex sign."

I took that as a hint, and I suggested that we go inside because the night had become cool. I had some wine in the fridge, and I poured two glasses of it. I wondered how I would gracefully go about unfolding the Murphy bed without appearing to be too anxious to get it on with Mary Jane. To transition as smoothly as possible into that scenario, I proposed a toast to the passion of Scorpios, to which she responded favorably by planting a big, tongue-mingling kiss in my mouth. I spun off the couch, and in one fell swoop I unfolded the bed and pulled Mary Jane down on top of me. We quickly stripped and began to screw so fast and furiously that I couldn't help finishing before she was satisfied. I rolled over on my back and sighed, unable to get it up again. But Mary Jane was forgiving, as most women usually were in the same situation. She kissed me on the cheek, got dressed and left, but not before she left a joint for me on the kitchen table. Feeling a little bummed out because of my poor love-making performance, I lit it up and took a couple of hits, along with a sip or two of wine, to console myself. I then lay down and gradually fell asleep.

In the morning I went back to City Lights to shmooze with Ferlinghetti. I wanted to know what he thought about the Vietnam War. I had learned that he was a veteran of World War II who became a pacifist because he had been to Nagasaki shortly after the atomic bomb was dropped on that city, and was aghast at what he saw. When I walked in, he seemed pleased to see me again.

"Find a place to rent yet?"

"Yes. It's not too far from here."

"You lucked out, then. It's hard to find something in this neighborhood. Everybody wants to live around here."

"Yeah. I'm told this is where it's at. By the way, Lawrence, I've been meaning to ask your opinion of the Vietnam War since you're a war veteran."

"Well, before I answer your question, if you don't mind, first tell me what you think about it."

"In the beginning I supported it, because I was concerned about the spread of Communism in Southeast Asia – you know, like in the Domino Theory. But now, after building South Vietnam up militarily and politically, we're about to withdraw from the war at a critical time, and leave them to fend for themselves against the ever-increasing presence of the North Vietnamese Army (NVA) in the south. I'm afraid the war will quickly become a lost cause."

"But keep in mind, it isn't a lost cause for the North Vietnamese," Ferlinghetti said. "As it turned out, we miscalculated their desire to unite the two Vietnams under Communism. After Ho Chi Minh waged a successful revolution against the French, culminating in 1954, he was elected president of one Vietnam, not the divided one that was mandated by the Geneva Accords following the revolution. The Accord, with U.S. support, nullified Ho's election and divided the country along the 17th Parallel, with the stipulation that another election would take place within two years for the Vietnamese people to determine if they wanted to remain divided. Meanwhile

Uncle Sam established a Western-leaning puppet government to rule the South, and the mandated election never took place. This led to another revolution spearheaded by the Viet Cong with support from the NVA.

"Have you ever read any of Allen Ginsberg's poetry about Vietnam?" Ferlinghetti asked.

"No, I haven't."

"In his poem *Wichita Vortex Sutra* he says:

*McNamara made a "bad guess" chorused the reporters in 1962*
*"8000 American Troops handle the Situation" Bad Guess*
*in 1954, 80% of the*
*Vietnamese people would've voted for Ho Chi Minh*

"And here I thought most of Ginsberg's poetry was about sucking cocks," I said, risking insulting his friend. He took it in stride.

"Oh no. He's much more versatile than that. You should read more of him. Which reminds me. Since you're from Springfield, Illinois, the hometown of Vachel Lindsay, you'd probably be interested in knowing that Allen considered him to be a forerunner of the Beats, especially because of his pacifism and socialist leanings. He advocated world peace and one world government, as idealistic as that might sound. Lindsay's poem *Sew the Flags Together* has a message similar to the one in John Lennon's song, *Imagine*. You may have heard that he was often referred to as the 'Prairie Troubadour,' because he traveled about the country on foot, trading his rhymes for room and board. Like Kerouac, he was fond of being on the road. And like Kerouac, he wrote about jazz and Buddhism.

"In fact, Ginsberg so admired Lindsay that he wrote a poem about his suicide. Let's see, I've got it here somewhere, in his collected poems. Where is it now?"

He scanned a section of shelved books.

"Oh, here it is."

Ferlinghetti thumbed through the thick book until he came to a poem simply entitled *To Lindsay.*

"I'll read you the last four lines."

*Vachel, I see your shadow on the wall*
*You're sitting in your suspenders on the bed*
*the shadow hand lifts up a Lysol bottle to your head*
*your shadow falls over on the floor*

"Spooky," I said. "But even spookier than that is a poem Lindsay himself wrote about his death, long before it occurred. I memorized it, but I won't burden you with the entire poem, just the first couple of stanzas, if you don't mind."

"No, feel free," he said.

> *I'll haunt this town, though gone the maids and men,*
> *The darling few, my friends and loves today.*
> *My ghost returns, bearing a great sword-pen*
> *When far-off children of their children play.*

"Tragically ironic, isn't it," I said in response to Ginsberg's poem. "That he would choose to kill himself by downing such a lethal drink when he was such a devout prohibitionist."

"Yes, isn't it? That's where Lindsay and the Beats differ dramatically. We tend to enjoy alcohol. Have you been to Vesuvio's yet?"

"Yes, I was there Friday night."

"Jack and Allen and I used to drink there a lot. In fact, they've got a special drink there called the Jack Kerouac. It's a small bucket of rum, tequila and orange juice.

"We also drank at Li Po's Cocktail Lounge in Chinatown. It's named for the ancient Chinese poet who loved drinking rice wine while communing with nature.

"Do you write poetry?" Ferlinghetti asked.

"Some."

"Then you should come to Vesuvio's Saturday night for the open mic reading. I'll be reciting a couple of mine. You'd be welcome to sit in."

Meanwhile, intrigued by what Ferlinghetti said about Li Po getting high on wine and writing about nature, something I did in the woods around Springfield, I spent some time during the week at City Lights brushing up on the Chinese poet. It inspired me to compose a nature poem of my own for the reading at Vesuvio's. It employed a falling autumn leaves metaphor to ask whether we followed divine plan or free will in our everyday lives.

When Saturday night arrived, I went to Vesuvio's early to get primed for the reading. Ferlinghetti was drinking at the bar. I sat next to him, hoping to get some encouragement, because I hadn't read in public before. I felt a bit intimidated in the company of a renowned Beat poet in a place where he, Ginsberg and Kerouac used to hang out. He put my mind at ease when he suggested that I just take a deep breath or two and have another drink, which he bought for me, along with one for himself. We toasted to the reading, which he began with a poem about Christ. Part of it went something like this.

*Sometime during eternity some guys show up and one of them...is a kind of carpenter*
*from some square-type place like Galilee and he starts wailing and claiming he is hip*
*to who made heaven and earth and that the cat who really laid it on us is his Dad*
*nobody really believes them or me for that matter*

Then it was my turn. I was still a little nervous, despite the booze I had consumed, but I bravely pressed on.

*When sun shafts pierce the chilling dusk,*
      *and autumn breaths a smoky musk,*
*I contemplate with bated breath,*
      *this question of the greatest depth.*

*When leaves fade,*
      *they spin, soar, float, dying.*
*Is it the whim of the wind,*
      *or a niched course drawn for tracing?*

Juxtaposed, the poems seemed to question the validity of Christianity and the concept of divinity. They caused quite a stir in the audience, which apparently included a believer or two. One of them, a big, intimidating man with a shaved head and a crucifix hanging on gold chain around his thick neck, angrily confronted us after the readings.

"What are you guys, anyway, a couple of atheists?"

"Agnostic," I retorted, "as I indicate in my poem."

"Listen, man," he said. "There are too many magical things happening in nature for there not to be divine influence!"

Ferlinghetti joined the argument.

"Does that magic include a man being born of an immaculate conception, and his resurrection after being crucified, when no one has ever come back to life on this planet? And if Christ was sacrificed and resurrected by God for the atonement of our sins, why is there still so much war, some of which is waged over religion – like the Crusades, and the wars in Northern Ireland and the Middle East?"

"Because, in answer to the question you ask in your poem, even though God has a divine plan for each of us to follow – the *niched course drawn for tracing* you refer to in your poem, he also grants man the free will, or *the whim of the wind* to determine for himself whether to engage in or refrain from violence," the man said to me. "If only we would follow the teachings of Christ, which is the preference for peace, then there'd be no wars."

In the end the debate ended in a stalemate, and *"....the question of the greatest depth"* went unanswered.

Riding the high I got from the reading, I bid Ferlinghetti good evening and headed out to Li Po's, which was rumored to be haunted by opium junkies who used to smoke the potent poppy resin there. Some people swore that the ghosts of the junkies still smoked it in the place.

Before going in, I smoked a little something myself, from the joint Mary Jane had left me.

The first thing I noticed when I went into the dimly-lit cocktail lounge, was a large, golden Buddha statue by the bar. A huge red and yellow lantern with golden tassels hung from the middle of the ceiling, and provided most of the lighting. Black – lacquered, teak wood-framed booths with red felt cushions. The booths were softly lighted by yellow-shaded sconces. Under a sheet of glass on the table of the booth I sat in, were many poems, written by Li Po, about drinking wine and communing with nature. I read one while waiting to be served.

> *We drink deeply beneath dragon bamboo,*
> *our lamp faint, the moon cold again.*
>
> *On the sandbar, startled by drunken song*
> *a snowy egret lifts away past midnight*

A pretty little Asian waitress came to my booth, and I ordered a vat of rice wine. While I drank, I read another poem.

> *Rinsing sorrows of a thousand forevers*
> *away, we linger out a hundred jars of wine,*
>
> *the clear night's clarity filling small talk,*
> *a lucid moon keeping us awake. And after*
>
> *we're drunk, we sleep in empty mountains,*
> *all heaven our blanket, earth our pillow.*

And then another.

> *9/9, out drinking on Dragon Mountain*
> *I'm an exile among yellow blossoms smiling.*

*Soon drunk, I watch my cap tumble in the wind,*
*dance in love — a guest the moon invites.*

After smoking pot, drinking rice wine, smelling intoxicating opium smoke and listening to enchanting Oriental music coming from places unseen, in my stoned state of mind, the golden glow of the lantern dangling overhead appeared as the moon Li Po wrote about when he too was drunk.

My head swam. I got up to leave, and the waitress caught me as I started to fall. She sat me back down in the booth, and brought me a cup of tea that she said would help to sober me up. It only made me higher as I floated out the door, but not before I learned the kind waitress's name – Lin Lo – and a phone number where she could be reached when she wasn't working at Li Po's.

Her willingness to give me the number surprised me, but apparently she saw something in me that she liked, even though I was drunk.

Perhaps it was because of the poem I wrote on a napkin that I gave her before I left.

*The Earth is yin, the Sun is yang,*
*together they give birth to woman and man.*
*though separated by millions of miles*
*they're the perfect distance between planet and star*
*for life's existence – so here we are.*

*But all the while I've wondered why,*
*is it a cosmic coincidence that defies all odds,*
*or a scientific experiment conducted by the likes of God?*

I knew from experience that marijuana alleviated hangovers, so when I awoke with a bad one in the morning I smoked some more of the joint I had left over from the night before. It also made me hungry, so I went to a greasy spoon down the block for breakfast. After I ate, I found a phone booth and called Lin Lo and apologized for being so drunk at Li Po's.

"No problem," she said. "Sometime Zen Buddhists get very drunk. You are like Zen Buddhist in poem you wrote. It's very Buddhistic in nature."

Then out of the blue she asked me if I had ever practiced tantric yoga.

"No."

"Would you like to try?" she asked.

I had heard of tantric yoga, and knew it involved sex, so, yes, naturally, I wanted to try it.

"Where? When?" I asked.

"Full moon tonight. Good time to do," was her answer.

I immediately thought of my courtyard. It was totally private, and we'd be out in the light of the moon. I gave Lin Lo my address, and suggested a time.

"Nine o'clock okay?"

"Yes, fine. See you then," she said.

When she arrived we sat at the kitchen table, and she explained the practice of tantric sex to me. I began to feel like I was entering a Masters & Johnson clinical experiment.

"If the intercourse is prolonged by going slow, without expecting climaxes, then you can just remain in the beginning. Excitement is energy. You can lose it by coming to a peak too soon. Then the energy is lost, and a kind of depression or let down and weakness will follow. If you can temper the excitement of intercourse without leading to a climax, if you can remain in the beginning without becoming too hot, just remaining warm, then you can prolong the act for a very long time. With no ejaculation, with no throwing out energy, it becomes a meditation and through it you continue to be one with your partner. When there is too much heat through intense and uncontrolled excitement, usually more than a man can handle, he boils over and discharges his life force too soon, disempowering himself.

"Making love is meditation. It is sacred. So while you are making love, go very slowly, there is no hurry, enough time is there. Remain for a while in the meditative state without ejaculation, to prolong the experience for the benefit of yourself and your partner."

I got somewhat aroused listening to Lin Lo describe tantric intercourse, so I proposed that we go ahead and try it.

"Okay, where?" she responded

"In the courtyard, in the moonlight. It's very private. No one will see us."

We took our clothes off and walked hand-in-hand outside, and sat down on the soft grass. She assumed a full lotus position and directed me to do the same. With our legs intertwined like two contortionists, we extended our arms and placed our hands on each other's shoulders, while smiling and looking into each other's eyes. We somehow managed to achieve at least partial penetration, and we held that position, moving ever so slightly. I was fully aroused, but I managed to control my excitement so as not to ejaculate, thereby prolonging the experience which Lin Lo had said was the goal of tantric sex.

After a while, the antithesis of premature ejaculation occurred: an old high school boy's bugaboo, called "lover's nuts." Stifling ejaculation caused semen to back up into the testicles, causing agonizing pain. In those days the girls would only let you go so far. What else could one expect from a half-assed fuck? No, tantric yoga was not for me.

I untangled myself from Lin Lo. Disappointed by my lack of cooperation, she went back into the apartment, dressed and left in a huff. At least Mary Jane had departed graciously although with her I had gotten too hot too quickly, and boiled over prematurely.

With summer coming to an end it was time for me to return to Illinois. I had hitchhiked halfway across the country without incident, except for the prank two mischievous teenagers pulled on me in the middle of Wyoming. However, I didn't want to push my luck hitchhiking back to Springfield, so I took the train.

I enjoyed the comfort of train travel instead of being buffeted by the grit-laden wind of semis roaring past me too closely. On the train I could get a cold beer in the club car. I took full advantage of that soon after we pulled out of the station.

I drank a couple, then went back to my seat and read some Ferlinghetti, Ginsberg, Li Po and Lindsay from books I bought at City Lights.

The clickety-clackety sound of the wheels on the tracks provided a background rhythm to their poems, which, along with the train's swaying, soon put me to sleep.

When I awoke at sunup, we were zooming alongside a cascading mountain stream. I assumed we were in the Rockies of Colorado.

I went back to the club car – this time for orange juice, eggs and toast.

The rest of the trip across the Great Plains was boring because of the bland scenery, and I dozed off while reading. We arrived in Chicago just in time for me to catch a train to "Springpatch" – a somewhat disparaging term some locals used to describe the Capital City's country bumpkin image Chicago's Mike Royko often joked about in his newspaper columns about downstate Illinois people. Personally, I was glad to be back among them.

In the end I had accomplished my mission to meet Ferlinghetti, who taught me that the Beats were hip to Vachel Lindsay. It was something that I wouldn't have otherwise discovered. .

The uniqueness of my education did little to persuade potential employers to hire me even though I now had a degree in Communications. Despite my being a Vietnam veteran who was a military war correspondent, the liberal media (which was mostly anti-military), wasn't impressed, so I was stuck tending bar again at DiLello's after graduating.

DiLello allowed me to drink on the house an hour or so before closing time at one o'clock, to prime myself for visits to the three o'clock bars with the intent of picking up women, but by then the patrons were either paired up, or drunk on their asses, so I'd just go home alone.

I was caught up in an endless cycle of serving and consuming drinks. My life was going nowhere. The future looked bleak, and my past had been bleak because of my tumultuous childhood and that fucked up war. From something I read in a men's health magazine I concluded that I suffered from a newly diagnosed syndrome called Post Traumatic Stress Disorder (PTSD). Its symptoms, the article said, could be alleviated with THC, so I bought some pot -- cheap Mexican shit -- and smoked it. In San Francisco I had smoked marijuana sparingly, so I wasn't cognitive of any long term, positive effects on my mental health. But now, in Springfield, I began to partake regularly, and my mood gradually lightened. I was able to function as a fairly content man who accepted for the time being bar tending was my lot, and my attitude changed from disgruntled to pleasant. But I grew tired of going to bed alone, so I made a concerted effort to remedy that late one night, by inviting a woman who came into the tavern on a regular basis to come home with me for a night cap after I closed. She consented without hesitation, and, to my surprise, when we arrived, she immediately laid out two lines of cocaine on the kitchen table with a razor blade. She handed me a tightly rolled dollar bill to snort one of them with, and I did it. It wasn't long before I was high. I felt like I was taking off in a jet plane and a tremendous feeling of euphoria washed over me in warm rushing waves. I began to chatter incessantly, and I couldn't stop clenching my teeth until finally my jaw ached, but that didn't keep me from talking even more about anything and everything that came to mind on what I thought was a highly intellectual plane. Apparently the woman felt the same way, because she nodded in agreement with everything I said and offered insights of her own. Just as rapidly as the words came out, our clothes came off, and before long we were fucking on the floor like two rabbits in the spring. When we finished, she dressed quickly and flew out the door leaving me strung out with a snoot full of snow. That was not the end of my experimentation with recreational drugs.

# CHAPTER 9

It took me at least two days to recover from the cocaine, and in the process I discovered that after being high on it I came down hard, like a crashing plane. In contrast, marijuana brought me down nice and easy like a butterfly. That's why I used it to treat my PTSD. It left me feeling mellow, especially when I mixed it with a drink or two.

I was concerned that I relied too much on booze and pot to cope with PTSD, so I decided to attend group counseling sessions at the local VA clinic.

I was surprised to see that the moderator was a woman. Her name was Donna. She had been a MASH nurse in Vietnam, I learned, when we took turns introducing ourselves.

Judging from the lifted eyebrows when I told them, the others were probably surprised to see an Air Force guy there who had seen action at Khe Sanh. We each had a story to tell that had contributed to our PTSD. Mine was unique because it began with my childhood, which was a contributing factor to the disorder according to the article I had read in the magazine. I didn't share that concept with the group because I didn't want to confuse the issue. War-related PTSD was more pertinent to that particular setting.

In one of the sessions, Donna revealed that on returning from her tour of duty in Vietnam, she became a protester because of all the gore she had been exposed to as a nurse.

"I didn't oppose it for political reasons. I was more concerned about the inhumanity of it all, having seen what men are capable of doing to each other in time of war. The slaughter needed to be stopped."

After attending a few more sessions, Donna informed me that she had become a psychologist specializing in dysfunctional family issues when I mentioned to her in passing that I thought that some of my psychological problems were related to my difficult childhood. Those difficulties weren't limited to me alone. My sisters had gone through what I had, and then some, as the females who remained in the household after our mother left. As I grew up, they were like mothers to me, mothers to themselves, and wives to my father -- taking care of the domestic needs of the household, like cleaning, shopping for food, cooking and doing the laundry. Besides all of this, they managed to get good grades and participate in extracurricular activities. After graduating from high school, Chris eventually married a loving man with whom she had a child; Terry remained single, earned a PH.D and became a professor of English literature, an astonishing achievement considering her childhood. I wasn't as successful. Like my parents, I succumbed to alcoholism and I alienated my sisters by showing up drunk at holiday gatherings, much as my mother did by phone. Chris and Terry sought counseling to address the lingering effects of their dysfunctional childhoods -- PTSD according to their psychiatrist. Because of my disruptive alcoholic behavior I was excluded from the sessions, and consequently we became estranged. I told Donna about this and she offered me individual counseling to specifically address my childhood. She gave me a card. "If you'd like to discuss it further, give me a call."

I had never talked to anyone about what I went through as a child, and I wasn't sure I wanted to now. I was afraid to open old wounds, and go through all of that pain again. Also I knew that to begin the healing process I needed to air them out, so I called Donna and made an appointment. After I told her about my history she told me that I needed to forgive my parents for their alcoholic behavior, because women like your mother, in the '40s and '50s, were under a lot of pressure to maintain a household, while your father, a combat veteran who had recently come home from the war and probably suffered from PTSD before it was diagnosed, was under pressure to support the household financially. As a result, they turned to alcohol to help them cope and the family became dysfunctional."

I had hoped to get some sympathy for being a victim of my parents behavior, but instead Donna excused it by contending that they were the victims of society, and my grievances were never addressed, so I blew the childhood/PTSD relationship off and concentrated on my war-related PTSD.

While attending group sessions at the VA clinic, I concluded that it was all about my frustration and heartbreak from seeing the men of my generation blown apart at places like Khe Sanh while risking their lives for the freedom of the Vietnamese, then coming home to see those of my generation protesting against them while exercising their freedom of speech, something that the people of Vietnam wouldn't be able to enjoy if the Communists prevailed there. As a result of realizing this my healing process began.

# CHAPTER 10

I continued tending bar at DiLello's, the most popular sports bar in Springfield, where the local rugby club held its notoriously wild post-game parties – whether they won or lost.

Goaded by the club's founder and team captain, Gary David Balmer, six players (three on each side) held a naked teammate aloft on his back and paraded him through the tavern while pouring beer on his genitals, a ritual common among rugby teams worldwide.

Balmer stood by laughing, apparently pleased that his team had attained such a level of legitimacy in the realm of rugby celebratory practices. It was easy to see why he was the captain of a rough and tumble rugby team. Though not a tall man, he was powerfully built. His leg muscles bulged and his neck and shoulders were like that of bull's, which served him well in a scrum. I soon discovered that he was more than a typical jock. One night, after last call, when Balmer was in the bar, as I was about to close up, he invited me to come to his place for a beer or two instead of going to a three o'clock bar.

I followed him in my car to his house. He drove a VW bus, the preferred ride of the hippies of the '60s and '70s. I hadn't thought of him being a hippie since he was into rugby, but the inside of his house looked like some of the hippie pads I'd visited in Carbondale – a hippie haven.

An antique floor lamp with a yellow shade cast soft light on the back and arms of a stuffed maroon felt chair that matched a maroon rug whose green vine leaves and yellow flower pattern were highlighted by the splash of the lamp's golden light.

"Have a seat," he said.

The couch that matched the chair looked inviting, so that's where I sat.

Balmer put a record on – the Doors – and lit a candle that rested in a saucer on an old travel trunk which served as a coffee table. On the trunk I noticed a paperback book by Jack Kerouac entitled the *Dharma Bums*.

"Beer?" Balmer asked.

"Sounds good." I rarely turned down a beer.

He went to the kitchen and came back with two green bottles of Beck's.

I noticed you have a book there by Kerouac called the *Dharma Bums*. What the hell is a Dharma bum, anyway?"

"Dharma is basically a Buddhist term for truth. The book is about the Beat generation trying to find it," he said.

"The truth about what, though?"

"Life, what it means, how to live it. It's all pretty subjective really. Life has different meanings for different people. Charles Manson sees it one way, Billy Graham another way."

"My girlfriend in Vietnam was a Buddhist, but I didn't learn much about it from her. Only the difference basically between the squat, pot-bellied smiling figure, and the slender more serious one you see in pictures of pagodas and temples. 'Happy Buddha' she called the fat one. Represents the care-free attitude of taking life in stride. I think she called the skinnier, contemplative one Siddhartha."

"That's right, Prince Siddhartha," Balmer concurred. "He was the true Buddha."

"So then, Buddha really did exist. I've always thought he was just a mythical figure, you know, like a Greek god."

"No, man." Balmer frowned. He seemed perturbed by my ignorance.

"Siddartha was born in the 6th Century B.C. in northeast India, the heir of the ruling royal family there. He left that life in search of something more spiritual and in pursuit of the secret to the end of suffering. At the age of 35 his pilgrimage took him to the Bodhi tree. Bodhi means enlightenment, which he attained there, and he spent the rest of his life teaching those drawn to the Path of Enlightenment that leads from suffering and dissatisfaction to spiritual fulfillment – in other words Buddhism."

"And that's what you're in to?"

"I'm in to the Zen form of it, really, which is Japanese for meditation, although I don't actually meditate. You know, like lying on your back and closing your eyes and deeply breathing, while tuning everything out, that takes too much of an effort, which defeats the purpose, I believe. I do it passively by being aware of life as it exists in the present moment. This is it, man."

"Far out, Balmer, I just got a rush when you said that."

"You got a rush from realizing it's true; the moment of knowing, or the knowing of the moment – a *satori*. It comes about naturally if you just let go of fretting about the past and the future and focusing on the present."

"Yes, but don't we have to plan for the future?"

"What we do each moment contributes to that. It's like when I'm working on one of my stained glass projects. I have a plan, but I don't worry about when I'll complete it, it's a work in progress as I focus on each cut, each solder that naturally leads to its completion. The process itself is free of the anxiety associated with fretting about when I'll finish, which is suffering, and suffering is what Buddhism seeks to relieve us from. That's the purpose of practicing the religion."

"How do you define suffering? I mean if you've got a toothache, you don't need Buddhism, you need a dentist."

"I'm talking about mental and emotional suffering, which comes mostly from dissatisfaction about things not being the way we want them to be. You may be dissatisfied with your car, let's say, for arguments sake, and I don't blame you," Balmer joked, and he laughed, "because it's old and it rattles. You want a newer one, but right now you don't have the money to buy one, and so you agonize about that instead of being satisfied at the moment with the older one, which despite the squeaks and rattles, provides you with adequate transportation. It got you here."

"So what's wrong with striving for something you want that's better?"

"To want is to desire, and desire leads to frustration when we can't have what we desire, Suffering results from unfulfilled desires and unrealistic expectations, like desiring some beautiful woman who is involved with someone else. Letting go of desire relieves us of the suffering and brings us peace of mind. Let go of the egotistical self which constantly desires to be fulfilled in one way or another. Let go of one's self, one's body – in other words one's life – without mourning for ourselves. Buddha taught that removing such attachments will ultimately lead us to Nirvana – Buddhism's heaven. Now do I practice all of this like a good Dharma Bum should? Hardly, I have too much of a desire for these."

Balmer held up his empty beer bottle and grinned.

"Yeah, me too," I said, "And it usually leads to suffering in the morning. I better go."

"Hold on, Mick. I've got something here that'll get you higher than the beer and it won't leave you with a hangover."

"Oh yeah, what's that?"

He smiled while dangling a baggie in my face that contained what looked like pieces moldy dried apples, but that was not what they were.

"Psilocybin – magic mushrooms," he said.

"So that's what they look like; not too appetizing."

"You don't eat them for the taste," Balmer replied, somewhat annoyed.

"Where do they come from?" I asked.

"My closet. I grow them in pressurized jars of fermenting brown rice. In the wild they grow on cow shit. Try one. Don't worry, it's not like dropping acid, if you've ever done that. They're organic, not chemical. The trip is much more mellow, I think: not as noisy, and it lets you down easier when it's over. You don't crash as hard. Go ahead, Mick, nothing bad is going to happen. Just kick back and enjoy the ride."

I took one and chewed it and swallowed. It was bitter going down.

Balmer ate one too, then he went to the kitchen and brought back two more beers to wash the mushrooms down with.

At first it was like getting off on grass. I felt light-headed and light-assed, with a quivery sensation in my stomach. I felt a little hot, then chilled, and the hair on the back of my neck bristled, and my scalp began to crawl. The saliva in my mouth thickened, and it was hard to swallow. I took a swig of the cold beer. Soon my entire body seemed to be levitating off the couch.

The music we were listening to – Pink Floyd's *Time,* driven by the ticktocking of a clock, sounded louder and clearer than I'd ever heard it before, as if the clock was in my head. And the lyrics, *...every year is getting shorter never seem to find the time, plans that either came to naught or half a page of scribbled lines,* made me think about the book I had planned to write about Vietnam, and how I kept putting it off, and I vowed to start on it soon – maybe tomorrow or the next day.

It appeared that Balmer was getting off now too, judging from the grin on his face and the sparkle in his eyes.

I began to see strange things. The wood grain in the arms of the chair Balmer sat in seemed to be moving like liquid beneath his hands, and the vine design in the rug looked alive and appeared to be growing all around his sandaled feet. The stucco walls seemed to be breathing and pulsating with the music.

Everything was connected by molecules and I saw that there was more to life than we seee in our normal state of consciousness. There was something below the surface – the underlying current of existence, that hallucinogens allow us to experience.

I shared my experiences with Blamer and he shared his in return, which were eerily similar. Were our minds connected too, by an underlying current of intense awareness, as in extra sensory perception, or was it just the result of the commonality of our experience of tripping on magic mushrooms together?

Whatever it was, it elevated my thoughts and ability to articulate them to new levels, and I realized that the time to live our lives was in the here and now, before it slips away, ... *and then one day you find that ten years have got behind you,* the lyrics of Pink Floyd's song continued to say.

"Far out! Now I get it! 'I exclaimed, "This is it!"

It was time for me to go home, but I was too stoned to drive, so I decided to walk to my house, about two miles away. On the way it began to storm so I sought shelter beneath the overhang of an archway at the door of a church.

Tired from being up all night, I laid back and just as my shoulder blade came down on an iron doorstop protruding like a spike out of the concrete, a bolt of lightening struck the steeple, and an image of Christ flashed before me. In my stoned state of mind I saw it as a cosmic message, with magic mushrooms as the medium, to turn to Jesus as the cop in Eureka Springs had suggested, so I went inside the church and prayed to Jesus that someday I'd reconcile with my parents by forgiving them for their trespasses against me, for forgiveness is one of the basic tenets of Christianity.

It would be difficult to contact my mother because I didn't know where she was, but I knew where to find my father – at a tavern on the other side of town where he was known to hang out. He was a small man who resembled Richard Nixon, except that he wore glasses. He didn't look like a combat veteran, but I suspected he was. Being a snoopy little kid I had discovered campaign ribbons with battle stars in a drawer at Grandma's house. I asked her what they were for.

"The Battle of Saipan in World War II. But don't ask your father about them, he doesn't like to talk about it. I will tell you this, though: his ship, a destroyer called the USS Phelps, won a presidential citation for the action they saw there."

I knew a little about the war from watching Walter Cronkite's *20th Century* on television. I was enthralled by what I saw – men in combat -- and I tried to imagine what that would be like. It wasn't a game that my buddies and I played in the yard. It was all about life and death. I could see it in their eyes as they approached Normandy in landing crafts on D-Day. Unspeakable fear, overcome by unimaginable courage as they went, undaunted, into action to save the world from tyranny.

That was in Europe. Dad was in the Pacific. That was all I knew, except for what Grandma had told me. He didn't tell me anything himself, and I didn't ask.

Eventually I participated in a war of my own – in Vietnam, where I experienced first hand what it was like to be in combat, in a hell hole called Khe Sanh. When I returned home, thankfully in one piece, I was determined to find out what role my Dad played in World War II.

I was convinced that he suffered from PTSD, because he had nightmares and he drank heavily, as did I, but World War II vets hadn't been officially diagnosed with PTSD. After the war they simply went about their business, working and raising families (resulting in the "baby boom"), while suffering in silence.

I thought that if Dad could talk about his wartime experience it would relieve the pressure he must have felt all of these years, keeping it bottled up inside, so I met him at his favorite haunt for a beer or two, hoping that might loosen him up enough for us to communicate for the first time in a long time.

At first we didn't talk about war. We talked mostly about sports and politics. He voted straight ticket Republican. Disillusioned with politics because of the Vietnam War, I didn't vote at all, which angered Dad. He said a lot of people had died for the right to vote.

"Remember, son, you fought for the right of the Vietnamese people to vote, too."

His argument made me rethink my lack of participation in the democratic process. We continued to drink, and Dad began to open up about what he went through in the war.

"After surviving kamikaze attacks in open waters, we steamed into a bay at Saipan to attack enemy artillery. The bay was lined with high cliffs. The Japs rolled a big cannon out of a cave and blasted our bridge, killing the captain and fourteen others. As we began to list starboard away from the island, our gunners scored a direct hit into the cave as the Japs rolled the gun back, thinking that the hit they scored would be enough to sink us; it almost did. Our return fire touched off their ammo and blew the big gun out of the cave and into the bay, along with a huge chunk of the cliff.

"Meanwhile we looked up at Marpi Point and saw hordes of natives leaping from a cliff onto the jagged rocks into the sea hundreds of feet below. They had been pushed to the brink when US

Marines and Army forced the Japanese army up the slopes on the outside of the island. I guess they were afraid they'd be killed by the retreating Japs so they chose suicide instead. Some of those who survived the jump swam through the bloody water to our ship, but we couldn't take any of them -- we probably would've sunk, the way we were listing. We just stood there and watched them drown, son. There was nothing we could do."

Dad dashed some salt into his beer, which he had mixed with tomato juice, his drink of choice. He drank it down and began to weep, draining himself of years of pent-up emotion.

Watching him suffer while recalling his wartime experiences hurt me too. I had my own war memories to deal with -- something I had begun to do by attending the veterans' group sessions. They were open to veterans of all wars, so I invited him to attend with me. He was reluctant at first, because he was from a generation that saw seeking therapy as a sign of weakness. He changed his mind when I told him that the sessions really helped me to readjust.

To enhance our healing process, I arranged for us to go on an honor flight to Washington D.C. to visit the World War II and Vietnam War memorials. Some Korean War vets who wanted to see their memorial were also on the flight.

We celebrated the tremendous victory our Armed Forces had won in the European and Pacific theaters -- Dad nodded in affirmation and smiled in proud response to what his Navy had accomplished in defeating Japan 30 years before in 1945. My visit to the Vietnam War Memorial was a little more solemn, if not sobering. I had come within minutes of my name being on that wall because I had just missed a plane that was shot down flying into A Shau Valley. There were no survivors. I stood before it with bowed head, and tears filled my eyes. The gleaming, polished black granite wall bearing 58,300 names of those who were killed in the war looked more like a tombstone, reflecting what some considered to be a defeat. Remembering what Dad said about fighting for the democracy of the Vietnamese, I came to see it in a different light. Standing before it became a healing experience for me, just as it had been, I was sure, for my father when he saw the World War II memorial. We flew home together feeling at peace. We'd bonded over our common PTSD afflictions – but I continued to grapple with two symptoms of the disorder – anger and alcoholism.

# CHAPTER 11

It's been said that nothing good happens past midnight if you're out on the town, and I found that to be true one night, when I went to a 3 o'clock bar after closing at DiLello's. It was a place called the Warehouse, and it catered mostly to those who had been drinking at the 1 o'clock bars until last call, so they were usually well on their way to getting drunk. It also catered to those who tended bar at the 1 o'clock establishments, like me.

Arriving relatively sober, I drank quickly to catch up with the crowd, which only meant that I got drunk faster. Unfortunately, I was drinking on an empty stomach, which intensified the effect of the alcohol on me. I tended to become combative under those circumstances, so I kept to myself as much as possible to avoid any conflicts.

While drinking alone at the bar I got into a conversation with one of the bartenders who attended the same PTSD group sessions I did. We were talking about the difficulties some vets faced in readjusting to civilian life after the war, when an intoxicated woman who sat nearby with a man, interrupted us by saying loudly: "Oh you poor Vietnam vets are nothing but a bunch of sniveling cry babies, always complaining about the way you've been treated since you got home. Boohoohoo, always feeling sorry for yourselves. Hell, ya lost the fucking war, didn't ya?"

That was all I could take. I splashed my beer in her face and a brawl broke out as the man she was with and I got into a fist fight, which spilled over into the crowd as those who'd overheard what she had said took sides.

The police were called. Because someone pointed out that I started the mele'e by dousing the woman with beer, police handcuffed me, took me to jail, and screened me for possible possession of drugs and a weapon. They charged me with simple battery, took mug shots and fingerprints and placed me in a holding cell with two other men. The cell contained a stainless steel toilet and sink and four bare iron bunks. I lay down on one of them to try to sleep it off, but the bunk was cold and hard, and I was kept awake by the other two mens' slurping and moaning and groaning. I guessed they were having some kind of sex, but I didn't dare look. I covered my ears with my arms until they were finished, then I finally fell asleep until the jailer brought us breakfast – powdered scrambled eggs, soggy toast, a carton of milk, and coffee. The other two gobbled theirs down like starving dogs. I only picked at mine, but drank the milk and coffee.

About an hour later the jailer unlocked the cell and escorted me to the booking desk.

"You've been bonded out," he said

"By whom?"

"Your bartender buddy at the Warehouse. He's waiting for you outside."

Before leaving I was given a court date to appear before a judge one month later.

What troubled me most about the whole ordeal was getting mug shots and fingerprints because now I was officially identified as a criminal -- just because I did something I thought was justified. The judge didn't agree – he slapped me with six months' probation and 120 hours of community service which I volunteered to fulfill by preparing and serving food at the St. John's Breadline. What goes around comes around. I had eaten there when I was hungry and living on the streets after I returned from Austin broke in more ways than one. I hadn't been able to work because of a broken ankle.

Volunteering at the breadline exposed me to a variety of interesting street people. One was a seedy fellow named Jim who occasionally came into DiLello's to buy a pint of cheap liquor with money he had bummed. As an aspiring writer of character sketches, I wrote a poem-like piece about him after I saw him walking backwards across a busy street in my neighborhood, flailing his ragged coat at passing cars. I likened him to an existential matador, tempting fate. When he reached the other side of the street unscathed, he grinned and doffed his crumpled cap and bowed while kissing his fingertips and sweeping his arm skyward in mockery of the heavy traffic he had deftly maneuvered through in his successful quest of escaping certain death. Then he spun around like a soldier doing an about face and marched off triumphantly to a dilapidated shack in a nearby railroad yard.

After I shared the piece with a literary fellow at DiLello's he told me that Jim had lived across the street from him years before.

"He was a fantastic young artist, but he refused to go to school, so his mother kicked him out of the house. She gave me some of his crayon drawings. Want 'em? My wife's been threatening to throw them away, she doesn't appreciate good art."

I arranged to get them, and I was stunned by how fantastic they were – masterpieces, I thought. A few were whimsical; one was of a topless, big-breasted Mexican woman in a sombrero dancing with maracas in hand. The one I liked most was a colorful abstract of the bloodied green face of a man suspended in space among asterisk-like symbols representing stars. A winding red road lined with street lamps led from the man's face through a hole in a wavy green ribbon wrapped around the cone-shaped head of a lady whose light blue face was made up like a hooker's. I framed it and hung on a wall in my apartment. It reminded me of a Salvador Dali in its abstract fluidity and dream-like surrealism. It was art conceived by a child prodigy who had gone insane.

The following winter was brutal, with deep snow and temperatures below zero. Despite the weather, I went to the Y one night for a swim to stave off cabin fever. Jim sat in the lobby. It was too cold for him to be in his shack, but he'd have to leave the Y when they closed, so, on the way to the pool, I told him where I lived, and that he was welcome to sit in a chair on the landing of the stairs of my apartment, a few blocks away above the health food store.

After my swim, when I went home and opened the door downstairs, I could smell the pungent roll-your-owns he smoked. He had accepted my invitation. I invited him inside and provided him a pillow and rolled out a sleeping bag for him in front of the fireplace, and lit a small fire.

Before he lay down he sat in a chair. Normally stoic, he muttered something when he spotted his drawing on the wall. He stared at it for a long time.

"Look familiar, Jim?"

He nodded and smiled.

"Haven't seen that for awhile," he sighed softly, perhaps pleased that his masterpiece had somehow survived, as he had done living in the streets all these years.

He took off his worn boots, placed his hat on the coffee table and crawled into the sleeping bag. Before long he was snoring. I went into my bedroom and slept well, satisfied that I had given this poor man shelter for the night.

When I awoke in the morning the sleeping bag was rolled back up and Jim was gone, except for the lingering smell of tobacco and body odor. I expected him to make a habit of coming to my apartment, but for the rest of winter he never came back.

In early spring we heard at DiLello's that Jim had been killed by a train.

# CHAPTER 12

Over time I became concerned about my drinking. Being a bartender kept me in the drinking culture. Tending bar kept me in the drinking culture. I started drinking around midnight every night (an hour before closing) to prime myself for the 3 o'clock bars, and then I'd wake up the next afternoon and have some of "the hair of the dog that bit me."

In an attempt to get sober, I quit tending bar and went on unemployment which gave me time to concentrate on writing a book. I believed that I had a book in me about my experiences as a war correspondent in Vietnam, especially because I was nearly killed when I missed that plane that was shot down in 1968, nearly eight years ago. I believed I had been spared for a reason, like writing a book, but I couldn't write it unless I cut back on the binge drinking.

Waking up sober in the morning was like the innocent childhood days living with my grandparents, when life was clean and clear, free of the fog of alcoholism. I was able to get a good start on the book.

To celebrate finishing the first chapter, I impulsively popped open a bottle of champagne – old habits die hard – and I started on another binge before I sobered up enough to write the second chapter. And that's the way it went for a while; write, celebrate, sober up and write some more, then celebrate again. The highs and low were like an endless roller coaster ride of highs and lows. If I was to finish the book I needed to end this erratic behavior; I concluded that I needed some outside intervention, so I went to an AA meeting. It was what they called a 12 Step meeting. At this particular meeting, they focused on the 11th step:

"Sought through prayer and meditation to improve our conscious contact with God as we understood Him, praying only for the knowledge of His will for us and the power to carry that out,"

When the meeting closed with our recital of the Lord's Prayer in unison, all attendees held hands in a circle with the other attendees. One passage struck me hard, *...forgive us our trespasses as we forgive those who have trespassed against us.* I thought about my relationship with my mother. If I was going to work the program in earnest then it was time to forgive her. The next time she called in the middle of the night, drunk, I vowed to tell her that all was forgiven, but the next time she called was in the middle of the day, and, to my surprise, she was sober. She had been for two years, she said, thanks to AA. She was pleased to hear that I, too, attended meetings.

The purpose of her call, she said, was to tell me that she was working on steps 8 and 9. In a sense, we were working the 12-Step program over the phone. Drunks were known to have a compulsion about talking in excess on th phone – even recovering drunks.

There was no doubt she'd changed. I could hear it in her voice – she sounded at peace.

In response to her desire to be sober, I was inspired to do the same. If a woman I considered an incorrigible drunk could quit drinking, so could I. I worked the program diligently, one step at a time, but I ignored the central concept of AA, abstaining from alcohol "one day at a time." Instead, I got ahead of myself and set a goal of remaining sober for an entire year.

On the 365th day, in a bizarre fit of "stinking thinking," I celebrated my year of abstinence by getting drunk. The relapse was devastating. I lost all confidence in my ability to stay sober. If I hadn't been able to do it through AA, it probably couldn't be done. I gave up trying, and continued to drink, but only occasionally. I was a controlled alcoholic who managed to maintain a certain level of sobriety -- enough to re-enroll in college to work on a masters degree in Communications, using what was left of my GI Bill eligibility.

I was delighted to learn that the book I was writing would qualify as a thesis, because it was creative writing, an integral aspect of the Communication curriculm. This was added incentive to proceed with the book, which might be published someday.

The first chapter was a reflection of what I felt while leaving the U.S. for Vietnam, and my first impression of that mysterious country after I arrived.

*Before 1964, Vietnam was just a foreign word I heard vaguely coming from the front room on our old black and white TV. We didn't keep up with the Joneses and I didn't keep up with the news. My head was buried in the sports page. Classic escapism. Counting Sandy Koufax strikeouts was more pleasant to me than hearing about body counts.*

*Ironically, that's where it finally grabbed my attention, in the sports page, when Cassius Clay proclaimed he would not submit to the draft to fight in Vietnam because he said he had no quarrel with the Viet Cong.*

*I soon became acutely aware of 'Nam when Glen King, a soft-spoken, hard-hitting guard on my high school football team, who opened holes in the line big enough to drive tanks through, was killed there. Ironically, while he was crawling through a bamboo thicket, the grenade on his belt snagged on a stick, which pulled the pin out.*

*Then Mike Gabriel, our team captain and a wrestler with Olympic potential, took some flak while flying a solo recon mission over enemy territory. Struggling to stay conscious, he wiped the remains of his leg from his face, applied a tourniquet and landed the plane safely. Now he's the captain of a wheelchair basketball team.*

*Tommy Joyce was next, the day before his baby was born back in the States. Then it was muscular*

*Don Schroeder, handsome Blaine Miles, wild Billy Martin and little Larry Whitis. One-by-one they fell, like dominoes, and my number was coming up fast. Uncle Sam's fateful finger was about to point at me, so I joined the Air Force, hoping to avoid combat. Out of a class of 50 at Armed Forces Journalism School, however, I was the only one with orders for Vietnam.*

*So me and 200 other shave-tailed nephews of Uncle Sam, soaring off into the wild blue yonder, talons poised, combat ready – to kill some gooks for God.*

*Taking off at sundown in a pink Braniff jet, I glanced back at San Francisco, partially shrouded in blue-gray mist. The Golden Gate Bridge, spanning the city's skyline, looked like a crown on the head of a queen watching her knights depart for a distant war. As I turned away, I caught a glimpse of light glowing softly in a tower on a hill; it appeared as a teary eye.*

*Settling in for the long flight to Vietnam, I wondered, which of us would not return? The baby-faced kid sitting next to me? The black guy across the aisle with an uncanny resemblance to Glen King. He was smiling with his eyes closed. Maybe he was thinking about a girlfriend, a wife and kids, his mother, or the joke his father told him last night over a farewell beer. Or the loudmouthed jerk behind me, yakking about how many "slant-eyed gooks" he'd kill? The Asian-American Marine sitting next to him? Me?*

*I gazed at my reflection in the window. My mother used to say I looked like Van Johnson, the war movie hero, with my reddish-blond hair, blue eyes and smattering of freckles, but now I thought I looked like some scared little kid on his way to the dentist. I could see fear in my eyes – fear of the unknown, and what awaited me on the other side of the big pond.*

*We leveled off at 45,000 feet above the Pacific and sped for 'Nam in a race with the sun hoping to prolong our last day of innocence. It was a race that we ultimately lost when the last glint of light was swallowed by the sea. We drifted all night, farther and farther away from home; and for some, perhaps me, there'd be no return.*

*A few hours later, we hydroplaned down the runway at Tan Son Nhut Air Base on the outskirts of Saigon, through a heavy monsoon downpour. The weather outside the plane looked cool, but when we disembarked, reality sank in. It was actually hot as hell, and within seconds I was soaked from head to toe with sweat and rain. Running would have been an exercise in futility, so I just went with the flow, and sloshed my way, one soggy step at a time, to the terminal building.*

*Inside, ceiling fans turned at a lazy pace as Vietnamese women, dressed in plain white linen blouses and black silk pants, shuffled about in flip flops, chatting incessantly as they swept up bits of trash and cigarette butts. Once in a while they'd pocket a keeper.*

*They looked so mysterious with their little round Asian faces peering out from the shadows of pointed straw hats. Their teeth were caked with red betel nut, a mild stimulant similar to chewing tobacco.*

*Soldiers wearing the uniforms of various countries rushed around trying to catch flights. I recognized the Aussies and New Zealanders because of their Bermuda shorts and bush hats, and they spoke English, of course. The Koreans' muscular builds, and stern, square faces set them apart from other Asians fighting in Vietnam. Cambodians, Laotians, Filipinos, Indonesians and Thais were harder to distinguish. They all looked pretty much the same, to me anyway: similar uniforms, complexions, facial features and stature.*

*Orders were being shouted in languages I could not understand, except for one, "Hey airman!" a mean looking MP yelled.*

*"Who me?"*

*"Yeah, you. Get your head out of your ass and fall in over here; on the double. Hurry up, let's go, can't fight this fucking war without you!"*

*After processing my orders, and a quick lecture on social behavior, "Use rubbers, they've got strange diseases over here..." I was sent to a bus and driven to transient quarters to await further assignment.*

*By this time the rain had stopped and a scorching sun shone. The bus felt like a sauna, even with the windows open. As we rode along Tan Son Nhut's busy flight line, I saw every kind of aircraft imaginable, flying in and out, civilian and military, loaded with refugees, soldiers and bombs, bound for combat or escaping it. A Pan American 707 lifted off with a deafening roar, and I saw someone's bare ass pressed against one of the plane's windows. The driver of the bus blew it a kiss, and shouted over his shoulder. "I spot one of those every time an airliner takes off for the World!"*

*"The World?" I asked.*

*"Home, man. This place is like another planet, compared to the States. They say going home is like going back to another world."*

*As a huge full moon rose above the base that night, silhouettes of helicopters and palm trees appeared before the bright lunar light. The mosquito net around my bunk softened the glare, giving the scene a dreamy look.*

*While drifting off to sleep I thought about home, and my buddies at Di Lello's Tap, and my girlfriend Rose Marie, who I last saw standing on the porch in the gloomy gray dawn just a day and half before, waving goodbye. It seemed so long ago, like another lifetime in another world.*

Oh yes, Rose Marie and that fucking "Dear John" saying she couldn't wait one damn year for me to return from Vietnam. In retrospect, I realize that letter affected my relationships with other women over the years. I entered them with the expectation that sooner or later I'd be dumped. It concerned me about my budding relationship with Cathy of Carbondale, who seemed fickle. I feared that inevitably she'd two-time me on a whim if I stayed around instead of moving to Austin when I did.

But since then much water had passed beneath the bridge that I hadn't burned, subconsciously keeping the possibility of at least a long distance relationship between the two us alive. I wrote to her to see how she was doing, and, much to my surprise I received a letter in return, inviting me to visit her in Makanda, Illinois, a small village near Giant City State Park at the edge of the Shawnee National Forest south of Carbondale.

"I bought a farm house and five acres of land with the money I inherited from my grandfather. I'm planning on growing organic vegetables and raising free range chickens and goats for the eggs and milk and cheese to sell at Mr. Natural's Health Food Store and coop in Carbondale, and I could use some help getting the garden started. Could you come down and give me a hand?"

Having been an urban kid who grew up in apartments, except for the short time I lived with my grandparents, I knew nothing about gardens – except for the tomato patch down the alley that I raided when I was young. Nothing like a sun warmed tomato straight off the vine, especially when you're hungry, which for me was most of the time. The cupboards at home were usually bare. I was raised for the most part, by an alcoholic father for whom buying groceries was low on the priority list.

Early in April, I headed south through Carbondale and into Makanda, where I stopped at a funky little general store and asked directions to Cathy Riggnin's place. The man knew who she was and he directed me to a lane that led to a house on a wooded hill. Her name was on the mail box.

Small green leaves had begun to appear on the trees. A smattering of red buds bloomed in their midst. It was a breezy, early spring day, cool but underlaid with warmth from the sun which shone in the clear blue sky. On a garden plot in the south hillside I saw someone pushing hard on a hand plow. It looked like a woman, probably Cathy. When she saw me approach, she stopped plowing and waved. I parked at the house and walked down the hill to her. She greeted me with a smile and a hug.

"Glad you could make it."

A big black Lab, wanting in on the action, wagged its tail furiously, and smelled at my pant leg, while two calico cats, backs humped, circled around my feet.

"You're just in time to help me spread the compost and manure. Bring boots?"

"Sure did. I'll put them on."

I went back to the car and changed shoes. Cathy guided a wheelbarrow up the hill to a wooden frame packed with decomposing material. She shoveled it into the wheelbarrow until it was full, then rolled it back down to where she had been plowing. I joined her, and, following her directions, helped spread the compost on the soil. It stank. Cathy mixed it into the soil with a rake, while I went for another load. When the compost had been thoroughly mixed into the tilled soil of the plot, we took a break. Cathy took off her boots and nodded for me to do the same.

"I'll show you your room," she said.

We went inside the house. Full of house plants it looked like a jungle. Cathy led me upstairs, down a hall and into a room. It was furnished with an old wooden bed, a chest of drawers, an easy chair and a night stand with a lamp beside the bed. There was a lush Boston fern on a glass-topped brass pedestal in front of the window. The cool breeze stirred the curtains and I was glad to see a quilt on the bed. I'd probably need it on these early spring nights.

"There's a bathroom across the hall," Cathy said. "Let's go downstairs for a bite to eat."

We washed up in the kitchen sink, and Cathy made sandwiches: cheese, lettuce and tomatoes with mayonnaise on whole wheat bread. She poured two glasses of milk.

"The cheese and milk come from the goats," she said proudly.

"Where are the goats?"

"Out grazing with the chickens."

"Chickens graze?"

"They're free range. I spread feed in the grass and they eat both. Makes for great eggs and a neatly-trimmed yard. Hope you're a morning person, Mick. I like to start work early, at sunrise. That's when the rooster wakes me up. Beware of that rooster. He's very territorial. He'll peck at your ankles all the way across the yard. He chases the cats too, and Sport, the dog. The goats head-butt and kick him, though, so he doesn't bother them."

"So what's next?" I asked, after finishing the sandwich.

"We'll plant marigolds around the border of the garden. They're natural insect repellents."

"What vegetables will you plant?"

"Lettuce, tomatoes, onions, cabbage, carrots, potatoes, beans, cucumbers and peas, broccoli and cauliflower, Brussels sprouts."

"Wow, you sell all of that?"

"At Mr. Natural's in Carbondale, and at a farmers' market."

"What's Mr. Natural's?" I wasn't familiar with the place from the time I had gone to school in Carbondale seven years ago in 1972.

"A coop health food store and café. They also have poetry readings and live music on Friday and Saturday nights. We could go there this weekend, if you'd like."

"Do they serve alcohol?"

"You can bring your own. Some people bring bottles of wine. I've got some bottles in the cellar that my neighbor traded me for goat cheese. We can take a couple of those – one for you and one for me. Well, let's get started on the marigolds."

It took most of the afternoon to plant the marigolds. It had become a warm day and I worked up a thirst. The first thing I thought about was a cold beer, but Cathy provided iced tea. We sat on the porch and drank it.

"Tomorrow we'll start planting. I started some of the veggies this winter in the house. The rest I'll start from seed. When everything is planted, we'll put straw down. That'll help control the weeds and keep the soil moist."

After baths and supper we played Scrabble long into the night. I grew tired, and tired of being beaten, so I excused myself and went to my room. I left the window open and lay awake for a while, listening to the sounds of the night -- sounds so different from those in Springfield. Having emerged from their winter hibernation in the mud, frogs trilled incessantly down by the pond. I heard the faint breeze in the budding trees, and an owl hooted in the distance. Before drifting off to sleep I thought about how much Cathy had changed, both physically and psychologically. I noticed right away, because she was wearing shorts, that she didn't shave her legs. Her hair had grown long, and her face was slightly weathered from being outside so much (her big blue eyes were just as bright and beautiful as before), but she wasn't flighty and insecure anymore. She seemed more grounded, and focused on her efforts to live off the land.

At sunrise I was awakened by the rooster crowing, and I smelled bacon frying. I arose slowly, sore and stiff from the work I had done the day before. I washed, dressed and went downstairs to the kitchen. Cathy was standing at the stove, cooking breakfast. I startled her when I said, "Good morning." She gasped, then laughed.

"Sorry. I'm not used to somebody else being in the house. Hope you like bacon and eggs."

After eating, we went out to the garden and worked for the rest of the morning, until lunch. We ate in relative silence, sitting on the porch and watching ominous clouds approaching from the west. There was thunder in the distance. A cool breeze smelling like rain rustled through the trees. Soon it began to pour.

"Good time to milk the goats," Cathy said. "I'll be trading a couple gallons for some more bacon and a pork chop or two with the neighbor down the road, who raises pigs. Bartering is alive and well around here."

We hurried through the rain to the barn as lightning cracked all around us. Thunder rolled like bass drums. Hail pelted the metal roof, making an awful racket. It was truly a severe spring storm. The goats were restless, but one by one they quickly calmed as Cathy sat on a stool and milked them. Despite the noisy storm, the goats' eyes, which normally appeared intense, were glazed over as if they were in a trance. The milk poured out in abundance, as she squeezed on their tits.

"Wanna try?" she asked.

"Uh, well, yeah, I guess."

"Here, sit down at this one. Now just grab one of the tits and pull and squeeze the milk into the bucket. Go ahead, it doesn't hurt them, in fact I think they like it."

Just as I began to milk one of them, a lightning bolt struck. It sounded as if it hit the weathervane on the roof. The goat jumped and kicked me, and I fell back off the stool into a pile of hay. Cathy began to laugh, and she dropped to her knees beside me. I pulled her down on top of me, and we kissed. We rolled over until I was on top of her. I forced my hips between her legs and pressed my pelvis hard against hers.

"No," she said, taking her mouth away from mine. "I'm not on the pill. Do you have a rubber?"

"No."

"Then we can't do this."

She got up and brushed herself off (I didn't need to, I'd already been brushed off) then finished milking the goats. She'd garnered about five gallons.

"With some cheese, this will fetch a slab of bacon and a couple of pork chops, along with more wine. I'll take it to the farmer right away. We can have the chops for supper. Tomorrow we'll have fish, if I can catch any in the pond. Because I'm Catholic, I'm in the habit of having fish on Fridays."

"Tomorrow is Friday already?"

"Yes, and I usually go into town on Friday nights to Mr. Natural's for the poetry readings. Mostly anti-war music and poetry. Not that I'm against the war any more since my brother became involved in it. But it's interesting to hear other people's perspectives."

Early Friday afternoon we finished in the garden and went fishing in the pond. We caught several sunfish and ate them for supper after taking baths, then we dressed to go to Mr. Natural's. Cathy wore a paisley-patterned linen dress and sandals; I wore a white cotton shirt and jeans. She brought two bottles of red wine from the cellar, and we drove to town in her pick up truck. The radio was tuned to an FM station that played soft rock. It went well with the beautiful rolling wooded hills surrounding the winding blacktop. I saw an occasional rocky outcrop through the hardwood trees.

We didn't talk much on the drive. The music and scenery obviated conversation until we reached the outskirts of Carbondale and drove past a stretch of strip malls.

"Like the song says, '...they paved Paradise and put up a parking lot,'" Cathy said as we drove into the old inner town where Mr. Natural's was located. We parked across the street. From the truck I could see through the windows that the place was crowded, but we found an empty table.

"I'll get glasses for the wine," Cathy said, and she went to the counter while I looked around. Through open double doors to another room I could see what appeared to be an old-fashioned grocery store. Fans hung from the high, ornate tin ceiling. A white porcelain scales sat atop a white porcelain and glass cooler. Packages of various kinds of nuts and dried fruit lined shelves, and wooden bins sat on the wooden floor. I couldn't see what the bins contained -- maybe potatoes, onions, rice and other staples.

When Cathy came back to the table, she noticed that I was looking into the other room.

"By midsummer a lot of my produce will be in that store."

Before long a bearded man with glasses sat on a stool and addressed the crowd. I was pleasantly surprised and especially proud to hear that he'd be reciting Vachel Lindsay tonight because the poet was from Springfield, my hometown. I had learned that he was popular with the Beats in San Francisco, and apparently also with the hippies of Carbondale.

"Lindsay was known as the 'Prairie Troubadour' back in the teens and twenties," the man said. "He traveled about the country on foot trading rhymes for food and shelter. He was also an ant-war activist during World War I, and he wrote poems protesting it. I'll begin with one of them."

The man recited a Lindsay poem one of whose stanzas impressed me

*To go forth killing in White Mercy's name,*
*Making the trenches stink with spattered brains,*
*Tearing the nerves and arteries apart,*
*Sowing with flesh the unreaped golden plains.*

In the trenches of Khe Sanh I saw many badly wounded soldiers and, indeed, the trenches were spattered with brains and other body parts. Lindsay's graphic poem was uncomfortable to hear. It paralleled my own war experiences, and caused my post traumatic stress disorder to flare up. My hand trembled as I raised the glass of wine to my lips and gulped it down, hoping it would settle my nerves. It did, so I drank some more. Cathy did too, and we were well on our way to getting drunk.

"Let's go back to the house and continue the party," Cathy said.

Back at the house, she brought another bottle of wine from the cellar, popped the cork, poured two glasses, and sat next to me on the couch.

"So have you learned anything about organic farming since you've been here?" Cathy's speech was slurred from drinking.

"Yeah, that it's hard work, and it smells bad."

"Oh, but it pays off so nicely at harvest time," she said. "And I can feed myself with it year round by canning. The potatoes, onions and carrots store well in the cellar, and I'm able to trade the goats' milk and cheese, and eggs for other things that I want. A pound of cheese brings in a pound of bacon; a dozen eggs, two pork chops and a bottle of homemade wine."

She clinked her glass with mine and drank. We were both drunk.

"I could use some help in the summer, harvesting, Mick. I'd make it worth your while."

As she sipped her wine she grinned and glanced at me out of the corner of her eye. Her body language gave me the impression that perhaps she was talking about something other than money.

In response to what I perceived to be a sexual innuendo, I said, "Why wait until then? I've done plenty of work already."

"This is true," she said. "I guess it's time for me to pay up."

We set our glasses down and reclined on the couch. I unbuttoned her dress and fondled her breasts.

"This is too cumbersome with our clothes on," she said,

so we stood up, undressed quickly and lay down again; two naked bodies intertwined, and I automatically slipped inside of her. Everything had happened so fast and in our drunken state of mind we didn't think about birth control as we had when we were sober in the barn during the thunderstorm.

Heedless of the consequences of our love making, we climaxed, then we both passed out in each others' arms, oblivious to the risk we had just taken.

In the morning I awoke with the sun beaming on my face. Cathy was gone. I went to the window and saw her watering the garden, and I concluded that there was nothing more I could do to help her. Everything had been planted. I packed my things and went out to tell her that I was leaving.

"I'll try to get back to help you with the harvest."

"Okay. Keep in touch, goodbye, Mick."

We hugged and I left.


A month later I got a phone call from Cathy. She was pregnant.

"I'm going to get an abortion," she said. "Since you're a part of the equation, I thought you should know."

"Hold on, Cathy, not so fast. Since, as you say, I'm part of the equation then I have something to say about it. I don't condone abortions, unless the pregnancy is the result of rape or incest."

"But it's my body and I choose not to carry a baby in it."

"Well, what about the body of the baby? You're just going to throw it away like a piece of trash?"

"Don't put it so crudely."

"How else can I put it. That's what you'd be doing."

"Let me ask you this then, Mick. Would you be willing to help raise the child?"

"I'm in no position to do that."

"And I am?"

"Your little farm would be a great place to raise a child," I said.

"Not without a father. If nothing else I believe in two parent households - a man and a woman. Studies show that it's conducive to raising a well-balanced child. Listen, Mick, just because we had sex once doesn't mean we'd be good partners in raising a child together. My mind is made up. I'm having an abortion with or without your approval!" and then she hung up.

Granted, when a woman is pregnant the embryo becomes a part of her body enveloped in the womb and connected by the umbilical cord, but at the moment of conception, the man is initially connected to the woman through intercourse as his sperm fertilizes her ovaries, making him an integral part of the pregnancy of course, thereby giving the man parental rights.

Thinking the argument would hold up in court I retained an attorney friend of mine. We sued Cathy to prevent the abortion. Because it was first case of its kind there was no legal precedent. If the judge ruled in my favor, it would be a landmark decision.


"But be careful what you wish for," my friend Bill advised. "Your parental rights could lead to parental responsibilities like child support, if she's prevented from going through with the abortion.

"We'll have to file quickly. Most abortions are done in the first trimester. If we can prolong the pregnancy past that, then there is a good chance the baby will be born. Then the question arises, who will be given custody? Could be a joint situation. Adoption would be a possibility if neither of you would be willing to raise the child."

"Adoption, huh? Now that's something I haven't considered. But of course Cathy would have to agree to give birth."

"We'll have to present her with that alternative immediately. If we can appeal to her maternal instincts, which I believe are inherent in most women, then perhaps we can convince her to continue with the pregnancy."

"I'll call her right away, Bill."

"I'm scheduled for the abortion at the end of the week, and to be perfectly honest I'm having second thoughts about going through with it. I can feel the baby inside of me – that changes things. I've calculated that most of the pregnancy would take place after the harvest. The baby is due in late December. If I decided to forego the abortion in favor of an adoption, I'd want it to be arranged beforehand so the adoptive parents could take the baby immediately, before I become too attached. As I've told you before, Mick, I'm in no position to raise a child, nor are you, but I don't want to kill it."

# CHAPTER 13

My mother, who had found religion through AA, called on Easter morning to remind me that the reason for the season was not bunny rabbits and colored eggs, but the resurrection of Jesus Christ. I told her about Cathy's pregnancy and the dilemma we faced – abortion or adoption. "Abortion is a sin," she said. It's murder. By all means, choose adoption. I'd be happy to adopt the baby," she said without hesitation.

"I'm sober now, and remarried to a loving, sober man. Toghether I believe we'd make good parents. True, we're a little older now, but we're also wiser. We've learned from the mistakes we made raising kids when we were drunks."

"Okay. Then I'll tell Cathy we've found someone to adopt the baby, and I'll have my attorney begin the required paperwork right away. I imagine the state's adoption agency will want to interview you and your husband ASAP. You'll have to come to Springfield for that."

Cathy was happy to hear the good news that someone would adopt the baby right after birth, depending on whether my mother and her husband were approved.

Cathy was due in late December – the 24th – to be exact, so my mother planned to be in Carbondale around that time. I'd be there too. It would be the first time we'd faced each other since she abandoned my sisters and me many years before. I was a apprehensive about the reunion. I feared the stress of the situation might cause her to relapse which alcoholics sometimes did, as I well knew. But when we met on the 23rd, I was relieved to see that she was sober, and she seemed resolved to what she was about to do.

A baby girl was born early in the morning on the 25th. Cathy gave her up without hesitation, to avoid bonding with her. It was a cold thing to do, but not as cold as having an abortion. I admired Cathy for choosing not to go through with one. When I went to her room to tell her as much, I saw that she was in tears.

"I didn't think it would be so difficult, but when my breasts began leaking milk my maternal instincts kicked in and I envisioned nursing the baby."

"Take heart, Cathy, someday when you're ready to raise one, you'll have another child. With someone who's a willing partner, unlike me, I'm sorry to say."

"That's okay, Mick, I wasn't so willing either. Besides, the baby wasn't conceived in love, but rather lust, fueled by alcohol."

Although I was pleased that the baby had been adopted, I was still her father, and I experienced a bout with depression and guilt over not being responsible enough to raise her myself, with or without Cathy. It was irresponsible for us to conceive a baby at all.

Because my mother adopted my daughter, I was comforted that I might be a part of her life. After only a week since the baby's birth I had time to consider the possibility.

Meanwhile the time had come to celebrate the beginning of 1981 at a New Year party at DiLello's. It was also the beginning of a new chapter in my life, and I resolved to finish the book in the next year, so I sat my ass down at my desk and wrote. By the end of February I had written several chapters. One of them follows:

*In early April in 1968, I walked along Tan Son Nhut's flight line and past a row of hangars, looking for airmen to record for hometowner interviews, I heard a special news bulletin blaring on Armed Forces radio: the Rev. Dr. Martin Luther King Jr. had been shot by a sniper at a motel in Memphis.*

*Several men, most of them black, congregated around the radio, waiting for more news about the shooting. I thought of 1963, when my high school principal announced over the intercom that President Kennedy had been shot. When we heard a short time later that King had died, most of the men bowed their heads, closed their eyes and prayed. A few stood up and strode away defiantly, muttering to each other about the good reverend being an Uncle Tom.*

*The whites, who continued working throughout most of the broadcast, stopped when Dr. King's last speech, delivered just the day before in Memphis, was replayed.*

*"Well I don't know what will happen to me now. We've got some difficult days ahead. But it really doesn't matter with me now, because I've been to the mountain, and I've looked over, and I've seen the promised land. I may not get there with you. But I want you to know tonight that we as a people will get to the promised land. And so I'm happy tonight. I'm not worried about anything. I'm not fearing any man. Mine eyes have seen the glory of the coming of the Lord."*

*Not even the cavernous hangar could contain his powerful voice. It blared all over the base in stereo as thousands listened to King's haunting words on their radios, but those words did not unite us in the aftermath of his murder. The next morning at chow, there was a pronounced divide between blacks and whites. They sat on one side of the mess hall, we sat on the other. What next, separate barracks, water fountains, latrines, separate bunkers to go to when the rockets came in? Separate units, separate nations? This was not what Dr. King had envisioned when he said, "I have a dream that one day, on the red hills of Georgia, the sons of former slaves and the sons of former slave owners will be able to sit down together at the table of brotherhood."*

*The night King died, Bobby Kennedy stood on a flatbed truck in Indianapolis and addressed an angry, grieving crowd. "Those of you who are black can be filled with hatred, with bitterness and a desire for revenge. We can move toward further polarization. Or we can make an effort, as Dr. King did, to understand, to reconcile ourselves, and to love."*

*When news of the assassination made the headlines of the Pacific Stars and Stripes newspaper, it was accompanied by stories of looting and rioting in more than 100 U.S. cities. In Washington D.C., Stokely Carmichael, the fiery black militant, called for armed violence against whites: "Go home and get a gun!" he reportedly shouted to hundreds of people in the street, while waving a pistol.*

*Hanoi Hannah (North Vietnam's version of Tokyo Rose) wasted little time in widening the schism. "The Pontius Pilates of American racism have crucified your peace-loving black brother. Rise up against them. Join the Viet Cong. Heed the words of H. Rap Brown, 'wage guerrilla war on the honky white man!'"*

*Thank God, such pleas went unheeded, at least in Vietnam, but it was a different story back in the world (U.S.), from what I gathered from the Stars and Stripes and various magazines. In Chicago, violence erupted, and Richard J. Daley, the city's no-nonsense mayor, gave police permission to "shoot to kill" anyone suspected of looting, rioting or arson.*

*Amid this disturbing news, I wanted to talk to my black coworker Bruce Samuels about how he felt about King's killing, and how he thought it might affect black/white relationships now, in 'Nam and back home. We met at the club, where, again, the division between blacks and whites after the assassination was all too apparent – in the way some people looked at each other, and even in the way we didn't look at each other.*

*Bruce and I wouldn't let it come between us. I shook his hand and said I was sorry, not in an apologetic way, but with empathy because King's loss was a sad thing for us all.*

*"I think he knew that was his destiny," Bruce said. "He said he might not get there with us."*

*"Where, Bruce?"*

*"That place where we all play nice together. In that promised land he had seen from the mountain the night before he was killed."*

*"Does such a place even exist, Bruce?"*

*"I believe it does. Don't you?"*

*"I don't know, man. Lately I've seen a little too much of that place where we don't all play nice together. My faith is being tested."*

*"Keep the faith, brother," Bruce said. "Just keep the faith. Say, by the way, did you know that I'm leaving on assignment for Khe Sanh tomorrow."*

*"Dangerous place."*

*"Yeah, so do me a favor, my man. If anything should happen to me, when you go through Chicago*

*on your way back to Springfield, stop downtown at Ebony Magazine and say hello to my folks. I've written about you in my letters. They know we're tight. Ebony's across the street from Grant Park on South Michigan Avenue, not far from Soldier Field."*

*"I think I can handle that."*

*But I couldn't handle the news we got three days later that Bruce had been killed at Khe Sanh. It hit me hard. I rocked back from the shock of it, and fell into a chair. I couldn't fathom Bruce being dead. Only yesterday we sat together at the club, discussing King's assassination. I put my face in my hands. I expected to cry, but I didn't; I was just too numb. Joe, the boss of Combat News stood there in silence, shaking his head, disbelieving what he had heard.*

*We closed up shop and went to Joe's villa downtown. We drank of course, and listened to some jazz albums in honor of Bruce, and to a tape we had recorded on New Year's Eve on which he introduced records as a D.J. in Chicago.*

*"From high atop the Windy City on a crystal clear mid-winter's night, this is Bruce Samuels, your host, as always, wishing you blue birds in the spring. But until then nestle with your baby near the fire and listen to Nat King Cole singing Stardust."*

Writing that sad chapter reminded me of Bruce's mellow FM style of broadcasting, which had influenced my style as a D.J. at the local university's radio station. Although my voice wasn't as deep and sultry as his, mine attracted a number of women to my listening audience. Among them, unfortunately was the crazy woman who had enticed me to smoke a pipe of marijuana laced with poison ivy. I'd vowed I'd get even with her someday, and as fate would have it the opportunity arose one night, when I happened to see her in a tavern. It had been a while since I last saw her; I assumed she wouldn't recognize me. My hair was shorter and I had no beard.

She was drinking alone at the bar, perhaps waiting for an unsuspecting man to hit on her, and I did, but I wasn't so unsuspecting.

"May I buy you a drink?" I asked.

"Sure. I'm drinking Harvey Wallbangers," she said.

"Bartender! A Harvey Wallbanger for the lady, and a beer for me."

"Thanks. You look a little familiar."

"So do you," I said.

"Lots of people say that. I've got a common face."

"It's a nice face."

I was making inroads quickly, perhaps because she seemed a little drunk. It would make it easier to persuade her to come to my place for a drink, and maybe a snort of what I would present as a line of cocaine. That was what she did the night she fed me poison ivy. The only problem was that I didn't have any cocaine – what a shame. I'd have to come up with a substitute -- something white and powdery, like baking soda, or laundry detergent -- anything that would cause her as much discomfort as possible as payback for what she had done to me. Even though I was a believer in forgiveness, an eye for eye took precedence in this particular instance. Laundry detergent – that would do the trick. It would certainly clean out her sinuses.

For the first time in my life, I welcomed "last call." It would open the door to the next step: getting her to come home with me, "... for a nightcap."

She consented to my suggestion without hesitation, and she followed me to my house in her car.

When we arrived I opened two bottles of beer, and we sat at the kitchen table. I looked out the window. It was snowing.

"Nothing like a little snow to make the night brighter," I said with a grin. "Care to snort some?"

"Sure." She grinned in return.

With her back to me I went to a cabinet, got two saucers and sprinkled laundry detergent on one, and some baking soda on the other. I placed them on the table, being careful to place the detergent in front of her. I cut a line of it with a razor blade, and presented her with a tightly rolled dollar bill to snort it with. She did, and I snorted a line of the baking soda.

"Oh my God, what is this shit!" she shouted, and she guzzled the beer flooding her sinuses, and soapy bubbles spewed from her mouth and nose. She jumped up and ran out of the house, snorting and coughing and choking and cursing. She poured what was left of her beer on my head, but it didn't dampen the delight I felt in exacting revenge.

# CHAPTER 14

In March my unemployment benefits ran out, so I had to go back to work. With the onset of spring, landscaping jobs would be plentiful. I hadn't worked as a landscaper since I lived in Austin, when I was forced to give it up because of a broken ankle. That was quite a while ago. Since then my ankle had healed enough to return to landscaping work. I didn't want to go back to bartending because it would lead to too much drinking. As of now, I had cut back considerably. I thought about spinning records again, but it paid so poorly in the Springfield market that it wouldn't be worth my time, whereas landscaping paid fairly well. Landscaping was a noble profession of antiquity, as I learned while reading some Buddhist literature David Balmer had given me during our magic mushroom trip. In ancient Japan, landscaping was considered an esoteric, Zen-like art form at least a thousand years before it was introduced to the West. It incorporated the contrasting concepts of Taoism in its creativity and practicality, sunlight and shadows, contrast of color and textures, size and shape, and contrasts in the contour of the land, all of which contribute to the totality of the beauty of the garden.

One day when I was scanning the help wanted ads in the paper, one in particular caught my eye. It was for a landscaping position at a nursery called Shinto Gardens. When I applied, the owner, a Mr. Yu Kubota explained to me that Shinto is a Japanese religion in which nature is sacred.

"Close contact with nature," he said, "is close contact with the gods, especially the sun goddess Amaterasu."

He said natural objects like rocks and plants, and even water, are worshiped for their spiritual essence, called *kami*.

When I told him I'd read about the ancient Japanese art of landscaping and its religious implications, he hired me on the spot.

Landscaping was hard work, as I knew from past experience. At times I was exhausted at the end of the day, but I didn't let that keep me from working on my book at night. After a hard day's work a cold beer tasted good, but if I wanted to write coherently I limited myself to just one, thereby striking a balance between indulgence and discipline in the spirit of Zen. It seemed I'd become somewhat of a Buddhist, but I was still a Christian, too, perhaps a Pantheist. I saw commonalities of many religions that worshiped an omnipotent deity: be it Buddhism, Christianity, Islam or Hinduism. The exception was devil worship – there was no room in my heart for evil. I saw enough of that in the war, leading me to ask why the benevolent, omnipotent gods of many religions would allow their followers to commit mass homicide. I addressed that in the next chapter I wrote, about a Chistmas party in Saigon to which my co-workers and I invited our Vietnamese friends for some international cultural exchange.

*The party began early at the Combat News office when Sgt. Joe, the boss, passed around shots of peppermint schnapps. Then we took a lambretta taxi to the villa, where a well-stocked bar and a fridge full of beer awaited us. On the way, we stopped at the neighborhood bakery on the corner from the villa to buy some fresh French bread for fondue, and to invite Pham, the baker and his wife Nam Nhu to join us for some yuletide cheer, though they were Buddhists.*

*Although our ostensible excuse for excessive drinking was to celebrate the birth of Jesus Christ, we managed to keep our revelry secular, at least at first, in deference to our friends' religion. Trip played his guitar and sang a medley of songs about good ole St. Nick, snow, sleigh bells and such, which delighted Nam Nhu, an educated woman who spoke English, albeit broken. Her face lit up like...well, like a Christmas tree.*

*"This Santa Claus, in sleigh, with reindeer, flies?" Pham, who also spoke English, asked incredulously.*

*"That's right." Joe laughed.*

*"And he lands on roof of house and goes down chimney with big bag of toys, says Ho Chi Minh name three times and puts toys under tree all cover with lights?"*

*"Ten four." Joe affirmed.*

*"What this got to do with Jesus Christ?"*

*Joe was stumped, but Steve, the new guy, had an answer.*

*"It's all about the spirit of giving, Pham. God gave to this world his son Jesus, who was crucified as atonement for man's sins. And Santa, well, he gives gifts to the children just to make them happy."*

*"This why 'tis the season to be jolly, fala-lala-la,' like Trip sing in song? And deck halls with bows of holly, don gay apparel, rock round Christmas tree while mama-san kiss this Santa Claus?"*

*"Yes," Steve said. "But essentially Christmas is all about the birth of Christ nearly two thousand year ago."*

*"Ah, then he just baby-san compare to Buddha, who is beacoup thousand years old. Who Jesus papa-san, mama-san?" Nam Nhu asked.*

*"Joseph and the Virgin Mary."*

*"Virgin give birth to baby-san? How so?" Apparently Nam Nhu knew the meaning of the word "virgin."*

*"Miracle."*

*"Oh, like reindeer fly?" She twisted her face into a frown, then smiled.*

*"I know, Nam Nhu. I find it hard to believe too," Trip said.*

*"You're not a believer, Trip" Steve asked with some surprise.*

*Trip thought it over for a moment. "I don't know, sometimes I am I guess. But explain this to me, Steve: If Christ was given to the world by God to save us all from sin, how come we still have war, especially religious ones like in Northern Ireland and the Middle East? I mean shit, man, that's about as sinful as you can get, killing in the name of God just because your neighbor chooses to worship him in a different way."*

*Without waiting for an answer, for which Steve looking puzzled seemed to be at a loss, Trip picked up his guitar again and began to strum and sing.*

*"Onward Christian soldiers, marching as to war, with the cross of Jesus going on before…," but then he took some liberty with the lyrics, "…and in the name of God they slay those Muslim heathens, who will surely burn in hell, because heaven is for Christians."*

*"Okay, enough blasphemy, Trip," Joe said. "Let's get back to the Santa stuff, and snow and mistletoe. It's less controversial.*

*"All right, how's this then?" Trip cut loose with a rocking rendition of Chuck Berry's "Run, Rudolph, Run," and the party rolled on well past midnight, until about two in the morning, when Pham and Nam Nhu, who had been drinking the rice wine they brought to the party, went home giddy and rosy-cheeked with a new appreciation of Christmas.*

*After a nightcap, I settled into my bed for a late December's nap, but I couldn't get something Trip said out of my dizzy little head. If Christ was given by God to atone for the sins of man, then why was there still war? Good question, Trip.*

*When the sun rose again, I still didn't have an answer, and I wondered if I ever would.*

# CHAPTER 15

While working at Shinto Gardens, I attended landscape design and horticulture classes twice a week in the evenings at the local junior college. I intended to go into business for myself someday. For now I was content to work for Yu. He enlightened me about the intrinsic aspects of landscaping through Shintoism. I came to appreciate the fruits of my hard labor as something spiritual in nature, which made the work more enjoyable.

I also enjoyed Friday afternoons, and not just because that was when we were paid. Nikki, Yu's beautiful sister worked in the office and distributed the paychecks. When she handed me mine I got the impression she was flirting with me. Perhaps she was simply returning the favor, because to be honest about it, I usually initiated the flirting.

We seemed to share mutual admiration. To follow up on it, one Friday when she brought my check, I asked her if she wanted to join me for a pizza and a pitcher of beer at DiLello's. She consented, and I suggested that we meet there at seven the following night. She agreed.

On Saturday evening, I dressed casually. I was surprised to see her dressed flamboyantly – in a black skirt with red flowers, and a red blouse. Her long, silky black hair reflected the red light of the beer sign on the wall above our table. She didn't wear much makeup, just a touch of lipstick and blush. Perhaps she was a bit overdressed, but she certainly turned a lot of heads.

I was probably underdressed in comparison – I wore jeans, a faded purple t-shirt and leather sandals. But we had plenty in common to talk about. Although she worked in the office, I learned that she had a degree in landscape architecture. She expressed interest in how my courses at the junior college were progressing.

"My brother is impressed that you're taking the courses. He says you have a natural eye for design, and if you get a degree he'd hire you as an architect."

"Well what about your degree. Don't you want to do some designing too?"

"I have – the garden around the house at Shinto. I designed that. Have you been in it?"

"No. I thought it was private."

"Not if I give a tour. Would you like to see it?"

"When?"

"Tonight. The moon is full. It will lend to the garden's enchantment."

"Okay. Eat the last slice of pizza, then we'll go."

"No, you eat it," she insisted.

"No, you," I said, continuing with the usual back and forth people eating pizza engaged in over the last slice.

"No, you."

"Alright, if you insist." I snatched it up and wolfed it down.

We met at Shinto Gardens, and parked our cars, and Nikki unlocked the gate. We walked down the driveway to the house at the back of the property, where she lived. At the entrance to the garden Nikki suggested that we take off our shoes to feel the coolness of the flagstones on the bottoms of our feet.

"Invigorating to the soul," she giggled. Her pun wasn't lost on me. We entered through a grove of blooming cherry trees resplendent with multitudes of pink blossoms glowing in the moonlight. She led me along a stone path, and across a bamboo footbridge that spanned a fern-fringed stream flowing slowly over round rocks. We continued down the phlox-lined path that meandered alongside the stream until we came to a pool bubbling like a spring. Reflected moonbeams rippled on the water. Nikki dipped her toes in it while holding my arm to maintain her balance, but the other foot slipped on the moist stone and she fell onto a mossy patch of turf, pulling me down on top of her. We lay there for a moment, looked into each others eyes and smiled. She giggled from the embarrassment of her awkward position. I was tempted to kiss her, but before I could, she squirmed out from beneath me. We got to our feet.

"Sorry I'm so clumsy, Mick. Maybe I had too much to drink. Better call it a night."

We went back to the entrance and picked up our shoes, and hugged each other good night.

"Thanks for the tour," I said.

"Thanks for the pizza, even though you ate the last slice," Nikki joked.

# CHAPTER 16

Monday morning when I got to work I poked my head into the office to say hello to Nikki. She nodded, smiled and waved, indicating perhaps that she had a good time Saturday night – an encouraging sign that perhaps we'd have another date in the near future. I had gotten kind of sweet on the woman, and while I was working, I couldn't stop thinking about her -- nor did I want to. When payday came around again at the end of the week, and she handed me my check, I invited her to come to my place Sunday afternoon for a cookout. My hibachi grill was just big enough for two steaks. When she accepted the invitation she volunteered to bring a side dish of rice and mixed vegetables.

This time she dressed casually in a halter top and shorts, and sandals that accentuated her shapely legs and attractive feet. I asked her if she would like a glass of wine.

"Sure would," she replied.

"It's red to go with the steaks. How do you like yours?"

"Medium rare."

I placed the steaks on the grill outside on the balcony and came back in. While waiting for the steaks to cook. I put on a Wes Montgomery record: cool guitar jazz. The music and the wine put me in a mellow mood, and it seemed to do the same for Nikki.

I went back outside to check on the steaks. They were ready to eat. The juicy red meat was delicious with the wine. I poured more after we ate, and our dinner party continued late into the night.

Because I had gotten drunk, I boldly asked Nikki, a Japanese Buddhist, if she had ever engaged in tantric yoga.

"No, I don't do it! What you think I am, some kind of geisha girl?" She sounded angry.

"Sorry, I was just curious."

"Curious about what? To see how far I go? I don't go far, not tonight. I've had too much to drink; better go now."

She stood, kissed me on the cheek and said goodbye, leaving me to wonder if our relationship would ever go beyond that level of affection.

Continuing a relationship with Nikki on a daily basis at Shinto Gardens, even if it were casual, would not be so convenient anymore, because after getting my associate's degree in landscape architecture and horticulture, I decided to go into business for myself. I had saved enough money to buy a truck and some tools and I had a few years of practical experience in landscaping. I was confident that I'd succeed.

I called the business *Johnny Appleseed Landscaping* and had that emblazoned in red on the doors of my green truck. I placed ads in the local papers and phone book and Yu was kind enough to steer my way any business he didn't have time for. At first I was able to keep up, working alone, but as the business grew I needed help. I advertised for an employee, and ended up hiring a couple of young Mexican brothers, Pepe and Jose Gonzalez who had green cards. They spoke just enough English for us to understand each other. I quickly found out they were hard working and conscientious, and accepted each task with enthusiasm. They had cheerful dispositions that lightened the physically demanding work, yet they took the job seriously when necessary. Pepe, the older brother, reminded me of Ramon, my boss in Austin. I expected that he, too, would become the boss of a landscaping crew, or the owner of a landscaping business, achieving the American dream of improving one's circumstances through hard work. And, like my friend Ramon, Pepe and Jose played hard, too. After work, especially on Fridays they'd grab a case of beer at a nearby liquor store, and take it to the campground where they lived in a small trailer during the season. Sometimes I'd get a six-pack and join them, and we'd build a camp fire around which we sat, drinking, cooking food and telling stories.

They told me about Jose sitting on a scorpion while taking a break from picking avocados in Mexico. The woman he was working with pulled his pants down and quickly removed the stinger from his bare rump to minimize the spread of the poison. It was an embarrassing situation for a teenaged boy. We got a big laugh out of that, but they laughed even harder when I told them about breaking my ankle while being chased by a cowboy on Halloween in Austin while I was wearing high heels.

When the landscaping season ended in November the brothers went back to Mexico, and I went back to working on my book. Day after day I pecked away on my typewriter until I had amassed a stack of paper comprising several chapters. Then I got a severe case of writer's block and I couldn't write again for quite a while. I needed stimulation, so I called Nikki and asked her to meet me for a few beers at DiLello's. I thought it might also stimulate our relationship, which had stagnated. It lacked the intense sexuality that I needed to satisfy my desires, so after a pitcher of beer I alluded to tantric yoga again, and again she alluded to the fact that we weren't married, so we couldn't do it. For me, marriage was out of the question, and for her so was any kind of sex beyond petting, apparently. Unable to find middle ground, our relationship ended unceremoniously that night.

# CHAPTER 17

Around Christmas, I was reminded of little Christine, who was born on that magical day one year before in 1980, and I wondered what had become of Cathy. I lost touch with her after my mother adopted Christine. Was she still truck farming near Makanda? Was she romantically involved with someone now?

Because my relationship with Nikki was over, I felt free to contact Cathy just to see how she was doing, so I sent a letter to the last address I had for her, thinking that she probably still lived there. Her roots were deep on that old farm. She was good at living off the land. We had that much in common: I made a good living landscaping and we both took the winter off. We'd both have spare time for a visit, so I proposed that in the letter. Two weeks later I received her reply, "...come on down."

The weather was mild for January in Illinois, so the drive down was free of ice and snow. When I got to Carbondale I decided to stay there for the night before going on to Makanda. I checked into a motel, grabbed a hamburger, and went to a bar called The Club. I'd heard that it was a Vietnam veterans' hangout. Many veterans were in college in those days because of the draft and the availability of the GI Bill.

At first it was hard to distinguish between vets and typical "College Joes" because nearly everyone in the bar had long hair, like most students did. I had known plenty of so-called hippie GIs when I was in Nam. In fact, I had written a poem about such guys.

> *It happened so fast after conscription,*
> *your transition from dispensing prescriptions*
> *at that free clinic in Frisco,*
> *to expending ammunition in a frustrating war of attrition.*
>
> *You became a GI Joe who scrawled peace signs on your hat.*
> *A hippie soldier you were called,*
> *although at times you experienced combat.*

*Peace and love might have been the talk,*
*when you were standing down,*
*and smoking grass from a bamboo bong,*
*but when it came to going after Viet Cong,*
*you went from dove to hawk.*

*Pundits like Cronkite claimed you were defeated,*
*yet you succeeded in kicking Charlie's ass*
*in just about every fight.*
*But back in the World you were expected to readjust overnight,*
*and become the peace-loving man you had been, again,*
*before you were drafted by Uncle Sam,*
*to kill or be killed in Vietnam.*

*And you did, despite an alcohol addiction and PTSD,*
*afflictions you managed to treat quite successfully,*
*with THC.*

There was a little THC going on at the Club that night, in a back room where a joint was being passed around. It was on the way to the rest room, so I stopped by for a toke or two. Smoking grass was a social thing done freely in a public setting, especially in hip places like Carbondale, where bartenders and cops, looked the other way.

Delightfully stoned, I returned to the bar and got another beer. One of the men who had shared the grass sat down next to me, so I bought him a beer for being so generous.

"Thanks, man," he said. "My name is Bill, what's yours?"

"Mick."

"Never seen you in here before – townie or student?"

"Neither, just passing through on my way to Makanda."

"I know of a hippie chick down there who grows some mean grass. That's what you just smoked."

"Good shit," I said. "I got a helluva buzz."

"Yeah. She also sells it baked in brownies at Mr. Natural's Health Food Store. Not your typical Ladies Auxiliary bake sale, but it's lucrative." Bill laughed. "When you eat one it gives you the munchies, so you eat another one. I prefer to smoke it though – goes well with these."

He clinked his glass against mine. "Here's to gettin' high," and he quaffed the beer.

"I see that you're wearing a POW/MIA bracelet. What's his name?" Bill asked.

"Timothy Bodden, from Taylorville, Illinois. He was a door gunner on a helicopter that was shot down in Laos. He's been missing ever since."

"Now that's a coincidence. I was shot down in Laos too. After two years of captivity, I was freed by a Marine recon patrol. We weren't supposed to be in Laos, yah' know, according the Laotian Accords, but we were responding to the NVA's presence there. Which was also in violation of the Accords convened to give Laos total political autonomy. The country was supposedly off limits to all foreign forces. At least that's what I've gathered from reading about it."

"How were you treated by your captors?"

"Not too bad at first, but after I tried to escape they got pretty rough. Slapped me around in the middle of the night so I couldn't sleep. If I dozed off during the day they strapped me to a tree and splashed water up my nose. Life can be hell when you're deprived of sleep."

"Bet you sleep good now."

"Didn't used to, too many nightmares, but then I got into pot. It helps a lot, along with a couple of beers. In fact, it's past my bedtime now, so long."

"Peace," I said, then I left too.

After a good night's sleep, I ate a big breakfast at a place called Mary Lou's, then I drove down through the wooded hills to Makanda to visit Cathy.

Although the trees were bare, their black, scraggly skeletons looked magnificent silhouetted against the gray sky like a charcoal rendered by an artist inspired by the stark beauty of winter's woods.

Cathy's reddish brown brick house stood on a rise among naked oaks providing a splash of color to the black and gray wintry scene. Smoke billowed from the chimney, signaling that someone was home. As I drove up to the house, Sport, the black lab, ran to my truck whimpering and panting and wagging his tail. So much for vicious watch dogs. The cats were nowhere to be seen, must have been sleeping as cats are inclined to do most of the time. Cathy came out on the front porch, smiled and waved. She met me halfway with a hug.

"Long time no see," she said. "You're looking healthy. Must be the landscaping."

"So are you. Must be the farming. Still selling your veggies and goat's milk and cheese at the coop?"

"Yes, and at a greater volume than ever before. I adopted a new way of farming after reading *The One-Straw Revolution*. Ever hear of it? It was written by a Japanese farmer named Masanobu Fukuoka. Come in, I'll tell you more about it."

"Man, sure smells good in here, like something baking."

"Brownies. I sell them at the coop too."

"Oh, I heard about them in Carbondale." I said with a chuckle.

"You did?" Cathy seemed surprise. "Where at?"

"The Club."

"Oh yes, of course. I go there sometimes to reminisce with the vets about my brother."

"How's he doing?"

"I haven't been able to tell you, Mick, because we lost touch for a few years. He was killed in Vietnam one day before we pulled out."

Tears welled up in Cathy's eyes and the mood darkened like a cloud passing before the sun, but through it all she managed a slight smile.

"Josh was planning to join the Peace Corps after he graduated from college, but then he was drafted. Ironic, isn't it? When they sent his body home they included the canvass cover of his helmet. He had drawn a peace sign on it."

There was a moment or two of respectable silence before I changed the subject.

"So what's this about your new way of farming?"

"Well, Fukuoka calls it the natural way of farming. He adheres to four basic principles in the process: no cultivation, the earth, he says, cultivates itself naturally by means of the penetration of plant roots and the activity of microorganisms, small animals and earthworms.

"Number two, no chemical fertilizer or prepared compost, which drain the soil of essential nutrients. When left to itself, the soil maintains its fertility naturally in accordance with the orderly cycle of plant and animal life.

"Three – no weeding by tillage or herbicides. Straw mulch, and a ground cover of white clover interplanted with the crops provide effective weed control.

"And fourth, no dependence on chemicals, because from the time plants develop as a result of such unnatural practices like plowing and fertilizing, disease and insect imbalance become a greater problem. Nature, when left alone with no interference with its natural process, is in perfect balance, Fukuoka maintains.

"As a result of practicing these basic natural farming principles, he has demonstrated that they produce harvests comparable to those of modern scientific agriculture at a fraction of the investment of labor and resources. So, where is the benefit of scientific technology, he asks."

While nibbling on the brownies and sipping coffee we gradually got high, and Cathy continued to tell me more of what Fukuoka wrote in *The One-Straw Revolution*.

"He says that long ago at the end of the year, the one-acre farmer who practiced the simple method of natural farming spent January, February and March hunting rabbits or relaxing before the fire, gazing at the glowing coals with his hands wrapped around a warm cup of tea. But gradually this three-month vacations dwindled down to three days indicating how needlessly busy modern farmers had become.

"One day while cleaning a shrine in the little village near his farm, Fukuoka noticed some plaques hanging on the wall. Dusting them off, he saw dozens of haiku composed as offerings to the surrounding land, indicating that the farmers of old had enough leisure time to write poems."

"So," Cathy smiled contently, getting up to rekindle the fire in the pot belly stove, "since adopting Fukuoka's natural farming ways, not only have I found time to hunt rabbits, but I've also composed a poem or two. Care to hear one?"

"Of course."

> *The sun-warmed turf of Mother Earth,*
> > *damp from the rain of a thunderstorm,*
> *germinates a seed in dormancy,*
> > *like the womb of a woman in pregnancy,*
> *giving birth to a tree in its infancy.*

> *And the question of the ages arises,*
> > *that has puzzled the wisest of sages.*
> *Which came first, the seed or the tree?*

"And for supper we'll have fried rabbit, with sauteed carrots and onions that I've stored in the cellar over the winter."

After eating, over a bottle of wine, we talked about many things well into the night.

Cathy asked about Christine and how my mother was doing with her.

"Everything is fine, last I heard."

"I hope to have a baby to care for someday," she said, somewhat forlornly. "But first I'd have to find a husband. Not too many would be willing to settle down on this little farm with me. Most men want a woman to follow them in pursuit of their careers in some city somewhere. Like you and your landscaping business in Springfield."

"Funny you should bring that up. I'm thinking about selling it to the two Mexican brothers who work for me."

"How come?"

"I've thought about doing what you're doing, you know, going back to the land. Somewhere down here in southern Illinois near the university in Carbondale, which would provide some culture – foreign films, lectures, music and the like. I'd be in competition with you selling my goods at Mr. Natural's."

"Oh, there'd be plenty of business for both of us. Are you serious about this?"

"Very."

"In that case there's ten acres for sale down the road from here. No house, and the land is full of stones, the soil is good though, in some spots, I've been told."

"Stones, huh? I've handled plenty of those landscaping. Who's selling it?"

"The guy's name and phone number is posted on a pole by the road."

"I'll drive down there in the morning and have a look. Meanwhile, if you don't mind, I think I'll turn in. It's been a long day."

"Suit yourself. You know where the bedroom is. Good night."

"Night."

I didn't go to sleep right away. I tossed and turned thinking about the possibility of buying some land down here. A lot would depend on how much stone there was and how much the guy wanted for it, and now much money I could make selling the landscaping business to Pepe and Jose. And what I would do for shelter because the land didn't have a house on it.

The stones! That's it, the stones. I could build a stone house. Maybe the Gonzalez brothers would help as a part of a deal for the business. But I'd cross that bridge when I came to it. First I'd have to find out how much the man wanted for the land, then I'd determine how much the brothers would be willing to pay for the business, and if they'd be willing to help me build a house with the cost of their labor as part of the package. My head was spinning with the possibilities. Finally I fell asleep until I was awakened by the smell of bacon frying. I got dressed and went downstairs into the kitchen where Cathy was preparing breakfast.

"Good morning," she said. "Sleep well?"

"Not too. Thinking about the land you said was for sale kept me awake. On my way back to Springfield I'll stop and get the man's phone number and give him a call when I get to Carbondale."

"Eat first. I wouldn't want to send you off on an empty stomach."

As we ate I told her how much I had enjoyed our short but sweet visit, and how inspired I had become about farming the natural way after hearing about Fukuoka's *One-Straw Revolution*. After a cup of coffee I bid Cathy a fond farewell with a promise to come back soon.

# CHAPTER 18

The acreage that was for sale was about two miles down the road from Cathy's place.

From the road I could see many scattered red cedar trees, indicating that the soil was very likely rocky. When I wandered over a knoll, a meadow came into view and judging from its expanse of green grass, it was fertile enough to grow crops. I plunged a finger into the turf – it was soft and moist.

Below the meadow was a pond into which a rocky stream flowed. The source of the stream, I discovered was a bubbling spring, which I hoped would provide me with potable water. I tested it by drinking some from cupped hands. As I continued to survey the property, I felt no ill effects.

Pleased with what I saw, I jotted down the phone number posted on a utility pole by the road. When I got to the general store in Makanda I called.

"Ten acres, $3,500." The man got straight to the point. "You one of them back-to-the-land hippies from Carbondale?"

"No. I'm from Springfield. I own a landscaping business up there, but I'd like to do some farming down here."

"This land isn't exactly suited for farming, although there is a patch or two of fertile ground."

"Yeah, I saw the meadow. It's about the size I'm looking for to grow some crops."

"You're gonna farm without a house, or at least a tool shed?"

"Well, as far as the house goes, I'm thinking that I might build a small one with all those stones on the land. And as far as tools go, the type of farming I'd be doing requires very few. Besides, I have some I landscaped with."

"So then, do you want to seal the deal?" the man asked.

"First I have to find out how much I can get from the sale of my landscaping business. I'll keep in touch. I hope the land will still be available by then."

"Okay, look forward to hearin' from ya."

Upon returning to Springfield I immediately wrote a letter to Pepe stating that I'd sell the business to him and Jose for $15,000 with an option to reduce that in exchange for the cost of labor he and his brother would charge if they were willing to help me build a stone house.

Two weeks later Pepe replied in a letter that he accepted my offer, but that he and Jose would only be able to help me build the house on weekends. The landscaping business would require their attention Monday through Friday.

"We'll stay in our camper on the land while working there on Saturdays and Sundays."

For shelter I would sleep in the back of my truck where I was protected from the elements by a camper top.

The cost of the brothers' labor was contingent on how many weekends it would take to finish the house. At today's hourly wages we estimated it could amount to about $2,500 for three months of weekends, or a total of 24 days of labor. Anything over that would be tabulated on a per diem basis.

Pepe agreed to pay me the asking price for the business (minus the $2,500 for labor), when he and his brother came north in the spring, so I called Ferd Weberling, the man selling the 10 acres, asking him to hold it until then. He agreed, if I would send him a $200 down payment, which I did.

In March, I drove to Makanda to pay the balance and sign the deed. While waiting for the Pepe and Jose to arrive I decided on a flat patch of sandy ground for the house. Stones were abundant nearby, and could be conveniently hauled to the site. Many were flat so I plopped them down on the sand to make a floor, which I completed in just one day. The brothers brought sacks of concrete that we mixed in a tub with buckets of water from the pond, to mortar the stone walls. We assembled three levels using stones near the site before Pepe and Jose had to go back to Springfield. By the middle of the week, I was able to complete three more levels with stones that I hauled in a wheelbarrow from farther away.

It was a warm mid-March day. The sun shone brightly, and I worked up a sweat and a thirst. Pepe left some beers in a net staked to the bank of the pond to keep them cool in the water. I popped one open and took a healthy swig, satisfied that I had made so much progress on the house in such a short period of time.

I sat on a big rock and looked out at the pond whose water rippled from a slight breeze underlain with the fragrance of some kind of blossom somewhere. Frogs, awakening from their hibernation, trilled incessantly. Spring had sprung, and so did I, up off the rock when Cathy came up behind me.

"Oops, sorry, I didn't mean to scare you."

"That's okay, I was lost in a daydream. So what brings you to Shangrila?"

"Just wanted to see how you were doing."

"Want a beer? There are some in the pond."

"Beers in the pond?"

"They're in a net staked to the bank. The water keeps them cool. Nothing like a cold beer on a warm day when you've been working hard."

"Yeah, sure, I'll have one. I see that you have been working hard," Cathy said, glancing at the early stages of the house.

I handed her a beer and she took a sip. "Ahh, I agree, there's nothing like a cold beer on a warm day when you've been working hard, which I've been doing plenty of all day.

"Hey, I'll make you a deal. If you'll help me with some of the chores, like feeding and milking the goats, I'll let you stay at my house while you're working on yours."

I immediately accepted her invitation. I'd have running water, maybe a hot meal or two, and a soft bed to sleep in, in the spare bedroom of course. That was unspoken but understood, unless things changed. There was always that possibility, I hoped.

"I'll meet you at the house when you're finished here," she said.

"Okay. It won't be dark for a few more hours. I can still get some work in."

"When's the last time you ate?" she asked.

"This morning, had a peanut butter sandwich."

"I'll rustle you up something more substantial for supper."

"Sounds good to me, I'll see you at the ranch."

Cathy drove off, leaving me enough time to set a few more stones in mortar before the sun went down.

When I got to her place, supper was waiting – baked lasagna and toasted garlic bread with a salad of bean sprouts (grown in a Mason jar on the window sill in the kitchen), topped with a creamy goat's milk dressing.

Because I was famished, I ate my fill without saying much until I finished, at which time I complimented her profusely on her culinary skills.

"If you don't mind, Cathy, I'd like to take a shower and go to bed."

"Okay. As part of the deal we made, could you feed and milk the goats in the morning?"

"Be glad to, if it means getting meals like this." I leaned back in the chair and rubbed my belly, stretched and yawned, and went upstairs.

I arose early in the morning, got dressed and went downstairs. There was a note from Cathy on the coffee maker.

"I had to go into town to talk business at Mr. Natural's. Help yourself to the coffee cake, non herbal. The goats are anxiously waiting to have their tits squeezed!"

I remembered how to milk them and how much they seemed to enjoy it, and I remembered how much Cathy enjoyed having hers squeezed, but that was a long time ago, things had changed, our relationship became platonic. Was that irreversible?

# CHAPTER 19

After nearly a week of working alone I welcomed the return of the Gonzalez brothers Friday night. They were amazed at how much I had done in their absence. It was time to put the window and door frames in place. Saturday morning we drove in my truck to Carbondale to pick them up after eating a hearty breakfast at Mary Lou's diner.

We spent the rest of the day and most of Sunday installing the frames and laying stone to the roof level, and because they didn't have any landscaping jobs lined up for Monday in Springfield, Pepe and Jose spent another night on my property. We built a fire, roasted hot dogs, drank beer and smoked a little weed in celebration of how much we had done. Later that night I returned to Cathy's half drunk and feeling frisky. I wanted to keep the party going if she was still up, and I was happy to see that she was, sitting at the kitchen table with a bottle of wine and a half-eaten brownie. Apparently she was celebrating something, too. She seemed happy to see me.

"Sit down, Mick, and join me in celebration of my birthday. Thirty-four years of staying single. That's not so easy to do in a society that expects its young women to be married with children by the time they're 25," she said, apparently mocking those who had.

"Guess I'm destined to being a fucking old maid." She drank more wine straight from the bottle, then she went down to the cellar and brought up another one. She popped the cork, took a swig and handed it to me, skipping the formality of pouring the wine into glasses. She took a big bite of the brownie and offered what was left of it to me. I gobbled it down.

"You haven't been married either, Mick. Don't you feel like a misfit too? Men aren't stigmatized with disparaging characterizations like "old maid," though. You're bachelors, which connotes independence, freedom to play the field, like a playboy."

"You sound a little uptight about it, Cathy."

"Yeah, well, you could fix that with one of your massages."

She turned her neck around and around and hunched her shoulders up and down, indicating that she needed one.

"Let's go into the living room. I'll lie down on the couch," Cathy proposed.

I began gently with slow, smooth strokes. Before long she closed her eyes, exhaled, went limp and fell asleep. Passed out was probably more accurate. She had drunk nearly two bottles of wine and ate most of a marijuana brownie.

I tiptoed out of the room and went up to bed.

When I woke up in the morning it was storming. Sheets of rain splashed against the window. Flashes from lightning strikes made me wonder what I was going to do about electricity and running water for my new house. I mulled it over while lying in bed before getting up to take care of the goats, and the answer came to me. I'd use my expertise in installing sprinkler systems to run a length of pipe in a trench from the spring down to a holding tank in the house under a sink. I'd install a pump (in the form of a faucet) powered by the electricity I'd tap into with wiring to the utility pole on the road. This would also serve as a pirate power source for lighting the house, until someone caught on to my shenanigans.

First things first, though. It was time to put a roof on the house, the last chore involving Pepe and Jose. They arrived earlier on Friday than expected, and we had enough time to go to the lumber yard in Carbondale for trusses, plywood sheets and shingles. We could get an early start on the roof on Saturday morning.

By sundown Saturday evening, we had the trusses and plywood in place and were ready for the shingles. We nailed them down early Sunday morning before it got too hot.

This concluded the gentleman's agreement I had with Pepe and Jose. I exchanged their labor for a reduction in the price of the landscaping business they bought from me. Pepe wrote a check for $12,500 and he and Jese went back to Springfield.

"Adios amigo! Muchas gracias!" they yelled cheerfully while driving away.

To make the house more livable, I put in a wood-burning stove for cooking and heating, and warming water for baths. I bought a stand alone tub, a bed, a table and chairs, lamps and kitchen cabinets from a resale store in Carbondale that salvaged furnishings from old houses slated for demolition. I bought bedding and kitchen utensils at the Salvation Army thrift store.

The last phase of the project involved the building of a small tool shed with an adjoining outhouse. I used old barn wood that I purchased from a nearby farmer because I was nearly out of stones. I could do this without the Gonzalezes' help. With their check in hand I was able to pay the $2,300 balance of what I owed Ferd for the land, leaving me a little more than $10,000 to live on until I turned a profit from farming by selling what I grew.

I got a late start with farming because I was so busy building the house. Cathy was gracious enough to help me get caught up by sharing what she knew about natural farming. It required very little soil preparation, except for planting clover for weed control. We chose varieties of vegetables that didn't require an early start, yielding a late fall harvest before the first frost. I grew green beans, tomatoes, peppers, cucumbers, carrots and potatoes, all of which were low maintenance crops, thanks to the clover.

A long, hot, dry summer in southern Illinois forced me to haul countless bucket of water from the pond to the garden, at least every other day. Cathy had to do the same at her place. The hard work paid off considerably for both of us when we went to market in the fall.

"In his *One-Straw Revolution,* Fukuoka discusses the marketing of naturally grown produce," Cathy said. "He maintains that growing produce without applying chemicals, using fertilizer or cultivating the soil involves less expense and the farmer's net profit is therefore higher.

"He says that other farmers in his neighborhood realized that they were working very hard, only to end up with less profit.

"As for the customer, the common belief has been that natural food should be expensive. If it is not, people suspect that it is not natural food so they won't buy it.

"Fukuoka feels that natural food should be sold more cheaply than any other. If a high price is charged for natural food the merchant is taking excessive profits. It is cheaper and less labor-intensive for the farmer to grow natural foods.

"If natural food is to become widely popular, it must be available locally at a reasonable price," he maintains.

Consequently," Cathy said, "Mr. Natural's is the perfect place at which to sell natural food products, because of the large counter-culture population in the area.

Cathy turned a healthy profit, and I did okay for my first year of production.

To celebrated a successful fall harvest, which was enjoyed by many of the natural food farmers in the area, Mr. Natural's hosted a feast and outdoor rock concert at Giant City State Park featuring the popular local band Coal Kitchen.

Attendance was not limited to farmers and coop members. Once the word spread that there'd be a party, people came from all around.

It was a breezy, but sunny day, and the fluttering leaves on the trees looked beautiful in their autumn hues. Their musty smell mixed with a hint of marijuana smoke.

The band set up in a meadow under a picnic shelter with electricity. Their music echoed off the face of a cliff from where frisbees were being thrown to those down below, who tossed them back up. Acrobatic dogs leaped after the spinning discs, twisting and turning like outfielders making difficult catches. They seldom missed.

Amidst the swirl of dogs and frisbees, people danced, and bottles of wine were passed around along with joints.

Cathy was among those dancing. I watched her from a distance for a while. She stood out in the crowd, perhaps because of the colorful paisley dress she wore. It fit her well. Farming had kept her in good shape.

We had been lovers for a few drunken moments some time ago, but now we were just friends, or at least that's the way she seemed to see it. Seeing her dance in the meadow aroused something more in me. I desired to be her lover again.

# CHAPTER 20

With the bulk of her produce having gone to market, Cathy began to can leftovers, including peaches with blemished skins that came from her orchard. They couldn't be sold to the finicky customers at Mr. Natural's. She invited me over to see how it was done. It was a detailed, but worthwhile process – preserving fruits and vegetables for consumption in the winter, and I enjoyed working closely with her on this domestic project. It made me feel more a part of a home than I'd felt before. I had longed for that in recent years, because I missed it in my childhood.

The kitchen was filled with warmth; a cold wind blew outside. It was strange seeing Cathy in a frilly apron – she usually wore masculine clothes, except at the harvest festival when she donned a dress. I couldn't take my eyes off her, then and now. She must have sensed that I was staring at her, because without looking up, she admonished me for not paying attention to the canning process.

"Sorry, I was admiring your peaches. They look so nice and plump."

She glanced at me out of the corner of her eye, twisted her mouth and frowned, but she managed a slight smile.

"Enough with the double entendres, Mick. "Let's get down to business, we can play later," which I took to mean that after the canning there was some fun to be had.

"Word games that is," she added. "I play a mean game of Scrabble, remember?"

Was she playing mind games by suggesting we engage in something as innocuous as Scrabble, knowing that I had been eyeballing her tush?

To prepare the peaches for canning, Cathy blanched the fruit in boiling water for half a minute, then placed them in ice water to cool them off enough to remove the skin. She sliced them into quarters, removed the pits and added lemon juice to the fruit in a bowl to prevent browning. Then she added a sugar/water concoction (which formed a syrup) to the peaches in a pot, and boiled the combination for five minutes. She then packed the peaches into hot, sanitized, quart-size Ball jars, leaving half an inch of space at the top, and poured the boiling syrup into each jar, screwed the lid and rings on tightly and placed the jars in a larger pot of low-boiling water for thirty minutes before removing them to cool at room temperature. After they cooled she stored the jars of preserved fruit on a shelf in the cellar.

Canning the tomatoes and green beans was a little more involved; a pressure cooker was needed for this process.

When we finished canning, which took more than three hours, Cathy got out the Scrabble board, poured glasses of wine, and we played late into the night until she complained about her chronically aching back. She asked for one of my signature massages. She was risking the potential for something more, considering how she turned me on. And her reaction to my previous massages told me that they seemed to turn her on as well.

Lying face down on the floor, she squirmed under the pressure of my hands that slowly moved from her back, over her buttocks and down her legs to her lovely little feet. Then I crossed her ankles and gently turned her over, a trick I had learned from a masseuse in Saigon. When I crawled up on top of her, she wrapped her legs and arms around me and we kissed.

"It's too uncomfortable here on the floor, let's move to the couch," she said, suggesting that we continue with what we had started. We had kept our relationship platonic for a long time, but suddenly, that had changed and we found ourselves nearly intimate again. This time, however, I came prepared, with a rubber should we go far enough to need one. But we didn't. Our move from the floor in the kitchen to the couch in the living room changed the mood and gave Cathy time to reconsider.

"We don't need to complicate our friendship with sex, Mick. It caused big problems before. Let's just continue to be good friends."

"We can be both – lovers and friends," I argued.

"But then you rob the friendship of its purity by placing so much emphasis on sexuality. I wrote a little poem about such things. It likens the lasting light of the sun to the purity of a platonic relationship -- which gives unrequitedly. The moon, which represents short-lived lust, robs the sun of its pure light, particularly when it comes to making love under the influence of alcohol when there's a tendency to be pre-occupied with self-satisfaction."

> *As wine flows tonight*
> *a lustful moon glows bright,*
> *robbing the sun of its pure light.*
>
> *And when the wine wears off,*
> *will lust endure until tomorrow*
> *in the sobering light of the sun*
> *a lustful moon has borrowed.*

I awoke in the morning, alone at home, with the sobering light of the sun shining brightly in my face. Through the west- facing window, a ghostly trace of the moon was still visible, its luster diminished by the brightness of the day. The lust I had felt for Cathy the night before had faded away, too and our relationship remained purely platonic.

# CHAPTER 21

Because I spent so much of the last year or so transitioning from a city slicker to a country boy I had neglected to work on my book. It had been more than 13 years since I left Vietnam in 1968, so I needed to get to it before I forgot some things.

With the onset of winter I had ample time to write again, and with the advent of personal computers and printers I was able to do so much more expediently than pecking away on a manual typewriter, using White Out to cover up typos.

I made steady progress, and by the first of March I reached what I considered to be the last chapter or two. To end the book on a positive note, I wrote that the protagonist, a Vietnam vet who suffered from PTSD, found peace of mind by going back to the land, getting married and raising children. However, before I got that far, it was time for early spring planting, so I put the book on hold again, until I could give it my undivided attention.

Throughout the winter Cathy and I each kept to ourselves. She was busy making quilts to sell at the coop, and I had been writing, but when spring came we got together to discuss combining operations to double production, hoping it would result in double the profits to be shared equally after we went to market in the fall. To avoid duplication we would select different varieties of produce to grow.

Even though we agreed to become farming partners, we stayed out of each others' way until an unforeseen situation arose that would bring us closer together.

I received a letter from Jerry, my mother's husband, informing me that she had died of a heart attack. This left him to take care of Christine, of which he didn't think he was capable at his age. He asked that I take her in, because I was the biological father. Cathy was Christine's biological mother. Whose responsibility was it then, to take care of Christine now? We weren't a couple. A difficult question that I posed when I showed the letter to Cathy.

She proposed that we move in together, and sleep in separate bedrooms while living as a couple otherwise. That way Christine would have both of her parents in the household.

I pondered her proposition for a moment. "Okay, then, I'm willing to give it a try. Let's shake on it."

"Like in Shakers – no sex involved," Cathy said. "But hugs are allowed. Christine should see some level of affection between mommy and daddy, don't you think? I mean, it's only natural, so give me a hug, Mick."

Mother was cremated and Jerry kept her ashes in an urn on the fireplace mantel in his house in Peoria. I cupped the urn in my hands and quietly recited the Lord's Prayer commemorating the close of the AA meeting she and I had attended regularly. I was especially drawn to a portion of the prayer that urged us to forgive those who had trespassed against us because forgiveness is what lead to the healing of the painful relationship I once had with mother. I kissed the urn and cried a little. But then I cried more when my sisters came through the door. They, too, had come to Peoria to pay their respects. It was the first time I had seen them in person in many years. We hugged and kissed. At last our estrangement was over, and forgiveness again won the day.

When it came time to take little Christine with me, she resisted and cried, confused about what was happening to her. I tried to explain that she was going to live with me and her new mommy on a farm. She calmed down and began sucking her thumb.

"Old McDonald farm?" she asked between sucks.

"Yes. E-i-e-i-o."

She giggled.

Jerry had packed a couple of bags with Christine's clothes, and he handed her a stuffed animal that she hugged, then held it up to me.

"Kiss," she demanded, which I did.

Jerry picked her up and gave her a tight hug and a kiss, then he sat her down and patted her little behind.

"Do you have to go potty?"

She nodded, so he took her by the hand to the bathroom. When they returned we said our goodbyes. There were tears in Jerry's eyes.

# CHAPTER 22

It was a long drive from Peoria to Makanda, requiring occasional potty breaks, and a stop at McDonald's for hamburgers. Jerry had given me a bottle of apple juice for Christine to drink on the way. While riding along she pointed out various farm animals that she knew, "...horsies, moomoos," and so on, until it got dark, and she fell asleep. Her angelic face glowed in the dashboard lights. I was able to find a St. Louis radio station that played jazz. The smooth-talking DJ reminded me of my radio days. Who could have foreseen that I'd end up being a farmer?

It was late when we arrived at Cathy's, but she had waited up. Christine was still asleep, so I carried her into the bedroom that would eventually be mine once the sleeping arrangements were finalized -- after I moved out of my house and into Cathy's.

Cathy lay beside Christine so she wouldn't wake up alone wondering where she was.

Because I had been drinking coffee, I was wide awake, so I sat at the kitchen table and read a book while waiting for Cathy and Christine to wake up in the morning. At sunrise they came out of the bedroom. Christine was rubbing the sleep from her eyes. When she realized she wasn't home anymore, she asked, "Where's mommy?"

Cathy squatted and took her hands. "She's gone to heaven, honey, I'm your mommy now. Are you hungry? Would you like some pancakes?"

"Uh huh."

"Okay. Sit next to Mick and I'll make some. After you eat we'll go pet the goats."

When she finished eating her fill of pancakes, Christine got down from the table.

"Go pet goats now," she said, tugging at Cathy's arm.

Cathy took her hand and they went down to the barn. I followed. Watching the little girl walk along, I was amazed at how she seemed to be taking everything in stride. I was just as amazed to see how readily Cathy had adapted to being a mother. It seemed to come so naturally. As for me, would I be able to assume the role of a father as quickly?

It wasn't long before Christine's typical two year old temperament emerged as tantrums that I found difficult to cope with. Cathy handled them well by not responding in kind. She accepted it as a personality trait of children of that age.

"She'll grow out of it," Cathy reassured me, noticing that I had become a little frustrated especially as the tantrums became more frequent. Perhaps Christine was having some difficulty adjusting to her new family situation. I was having second thoughts about moving in with the them, but I was the little girls father, so I decided it was the right thing to do. I moved out of my little stone house, and advertised it for rent in the Carbondale paper, thinking it would appeal to some hippie there. I'd continue farming the land as a tenant farmer in reverse.

As Cathy had anticipated, Christine grew out of the "terrible twos" around the time she turned three, and the dynamics of our relationship changed, almost overnight. She began to call me Daddy, and a special bond developed between us — naturally, as father and daughter. It was I who tucked her in every night after reading her stories and leading her in the bedtime prayer that my grandmother and I used to recite in unison while kneeling beside the bed. *Now I lay me down to sleep, I pray the Lord my soul to keep and if I die before I wake, I pray the Lord my soul to take.*

Cathy had fixed up one of the bedrooms for me, and she converted the little sewing room into a bedroom for Christine, who grew accustomed to sleeping by herself, as did I, having done it for so long. Occasionally the urge to sleep with Cathy came over me. After all, we were living as father and mother, why not husband and wife, even though we weren't married? Why not, indeed? The reason for sleeping separately derived from Cathy's fear of becoming pregnant again, so when she mentioned that because she had adapted so well to motherhood, she'd like to have another baby -- but not without being married. Our sleeping arrangement continued status quo.

One afternoon as Christine napped and Cathy and I sat at the kitchen table drinking coffee and discussing our farming partnership, she suddenly opened up about our relationship.

"Mick, I must say you've shown yourself to be a good father to Christine, and when you moved in you displayed the characteristics I've always looked for in a husband."

She put her hands on mine and looked deep into my eyes.

"I've grown to love you, Mick. Do you love me?"

"Yes I do. I have for quite some time."

We stood up, embraced and kissed longingly, like a man and a woman who had finally come together after suppressing their desires for a very long time. Then, as if we were dancing, I spun Cathy around toward her bedroom door, but she resisted.

"I'm an old fashioned girl now, let's wait until we're married."

"But we've already done it, remember? Christine is proof of that."

"Well yes, of course, but I was awfully drunk. I want to start over, fresh and sober, when we're married."

"And when will that be?"

"How about some time in June. That'll give us a couple of months to plan. I'd like to keep it simple. There's a lovely little stone chapel about three miles from here that would be ideal for a small wedding. The pastor and his wife shop at Mr. Natural's. I could talk to him about reserving it, and presiding over ours. What do you think?"

"Sounds fine to me. I'll design the invitations on my computer once we've set an exact time and date."

"I'll discuss all of that with the pastor. We'll have the reception here at the house."

# CHAPTER 23

June 10 was the day on which Cathy and Pastor Thomas Grey decided for the wedding at "The Stone Chapel on the Hill." Mrs. Grey played the piano. Pepe Gonzalez was my best man, and a woman named Sally, a friend of Cathy's from Mr. Natural's, was her bridesmaid. Sally's son carried the ring on a decorative cushion, and Christine carried a basket of flowers in the procession.

Cathy looked lovely from head to toe in a low cut, full length lacy white linen dress with strappy white sandals.

Sunbeams shining through a stained glass window splashed golden light on Cathy's smiling face as we recited our vows.

At the reception at the house, Pepe offered shots of tequila to those who were bold enough to partake. Homemade wine was provided for everyone by a man from Mr. Natural's, and Cathy provided goat cheese and her signature herbal brownies to go along with the wine as a appetite stimulus. She made it clear, for the benefit of those who didn't get high, before serving the brownies that they were of the potent variety.

There was a buffet of roasted free range chicken, stewed rabbit, and fried fish from the pond, with a variety of fresh vegetables.

After eating, Sally and two other women played music with a fiddle, guitar and tambourine, and they sang as the wine flowed freely, but Cathy and I abstained. As newlyweds we wanted to be sober when it was time to consummate our marriage.

When everyone had left later that night, and when Christine was fast asleep in her bed, we made sweet love in our bed like we had never done before — as husband and wife.

Nine months later a boy named Joshua was born.

# THE END

Printed in the United States
By Bookmasters